He studied
"Sarah, what's w
"Nothing,

talk about someth...g ..... .
It'll only make us feel worse."

"But what if it brings some healing?" he pointed
out.

"Since when do you want to talk about feelings?"
she argued, "I seem to remember you hating any
conversation that even remotely revolved around the
topic."

"Well, that's before I saw you standing out here
crying," he reasoned, "If I can help, I'd like to."

New tears welled in her eyes, and she shook her
head in an effort to keep him from seeing them. "Oh,
Cade, I wish you could," she admitted before rushing
back into the restaurant and into the ladies' bathroom.

ABOUT THE AUTHOR

Kayla Freshcorn discovered a love for writing years ago, and under her pen name M. R. Freshcorn, she has written and published several books on Amazon including the Skyrunners Series, a sci-fi adventure for 10-15 year olds, and The Adventures Of Billy The Kid, a bedtime story for kids about a baby goat. It has been her dream to become an author, and she hopes her books bring joy to her readers and also glory to God. She hopes to inspire others to follow their dreams because there is nothing impossible for God. She continues to write surrounded by her family, cats, and dogs, and she has plans for many more books. If you would like to stay informed on new releases and more, follow her on Twitter @M_R_Freshcorn525.

Books By This Author:

The Skyrunners Series:
Rescue Kit
The Royal Mishap
Hunted

Billy The Kid's Big Adventure

The Short Story Collection Volume 1

The Horse Whisperer's

Second Chance

Kayla Freshcorn

KayLaReigh

"Forget the former things; do not dwell on the past. See, I am doing a new thing! Now it springs up; do you not perceive it? I am making a way in the wilderness and streams in the wasteland."

Isaiah 43:18-19

To God, thank you for helping me each step

of the way on this incredible journey!

And to my family, thank you for all your love and your support!

I couldn't have done it without you!

CHAPTER ONE

Sarah Makenna inhaled deeply to try to calm her nerves as she mentally prepared herself for this next challenge. It was going to be hard, but she could do it. She would have to. There was no other choice.

After she put her CRV in park, she turned around in her seat to face her little nine year old nephew, Josh, who was staring down at his phone, watching some cartoons.

"Alright, Josh, remember," she reminded him, "This interview is very important. If I get this job, I'll have more time to spend with you than I did before at the restaurant."

Josh looked up at her and shrugged. "So?"

She frowned, but undaunted, she tried again.

"Also, if I get this job, we'll get to stay on this ranch, and you'll—"

"Will I get to see some horses!?" he exclaimed, suddenly springing to life, so much so that he made her jump slightly.

She chuckled and nodded. "Yes, you'll be able to see some horses, but..." Her voice got firm at this point. "You'll only be able to look at them. I don't want you riding them until you're much older."

He harrumphed and crossed his arms, grumbling something about if he wanted to ride horses, he could ride horses.

"Josh..." She stressed his name.

"Fine, whatever." Josh shrugged.

She blew out a breath that caused a loose strand of hair to fly up with the gust. Her watch buzzed, telling her it was time to head in for her interview. Reluctantly, she would just have to leave the argument there. Reaching for the door handle, she stated, "Alright, it's time for us to head in. Come on."

He opened his door and headed out without saying anything else to her. She frowned and glanced up at the sky. Was this what it was like being a mom? It was not easy.

"Wild Hearts Ranch," Josh read the words on the metal archway over the path they were about to take, and she nodded.

"That's the name of the ranch," she replied, "Pretty cool, right?"

"I guess," he muttered, obviously still mad about the horse thing.

She bit her lower lip. Maybe it was a bad idea bringing him here. With his bloodline, this could be a big mistake. Yet, something about ranch life was calling her home. Oh, how she had missed it all these long years away in the big city, and she knew it would do Josh some good too. She just wondered if she was capable enough as a mom to handle his stubborn streak. She had a feeling he was going to test her to her limits.

"Come on," she replied, nudging him forwards, "Let's keep going. We don't want to be late."

As they neared the main office, fear suddenly began to nag at her. What if Josh started misbehaving in front of Mr. Martin, the man who owned this place. Would he disqualify her for that? Josh knew how important this was though, she reminded herself. Surely, he would at least try to behave. She frowned. This was

Josh she was thinking about. Perhaps, one more reminder wouldn't hurt.

"Now, remember, Josh. It's very unusual for kids to come to their parent's job interview, but the Martins' were kind enough to say you could tag along since I couldn't find a babysitter on such short notice. That means it's very important for you to be on your best behavior, alright?"

"You're not my parent." His cutting remark tore through her like a knife, cutting her deep.

Ever since her sister and brother-in-law's accident, she had hoped that she and Josh could become a family, but he was so resistant to the idea. She understood why, but that didn't mean that it didn't hurt.

She squared her shoulders and shook her head. No, she wasn't going to dwell on that. She had her and Josh's future to think about. She needed to keep her head focused on the here and now if she hoped to continue providing for Josh as he deserved.

She marched on towards the main office and motioned for Josh to keep up, but he trudged along behind her, kicking at the rocks on the dirt pathway that led from the parking area to the main office and all the barns and stables beyond.

As they were just about to reach the steps of the main office, Sarah was stopped by a friendly hello called from over to her left. She turned around to find an older man walking up from the stables and waving at them.

"You must be Miss Makenna!" he called to her as he closed the distance between them, "I'm Henry Martin."

He offered her his hand, and she shook it.

"Nice to meet you," she replied, "Thank you for considering me for this position and for letting Josh tag along too. I know it's not the most orthodox thing, but I really do appreciate it."

He scoffed at that and dismissed her with a wave. "Oh, don't worry about it. It's not like we're super uptight here. No one'll care. Everyone's pretty laid back on our team. Plus, it's always fun to have a young-en around. It keeps things interesting. Besides, if you get the job as our cook, he'll have to live here too, right? He might as well get a look see himself."

She nodded with a smile as her shoulders relaxed slightly, grateful he felt that way about it. "Yea, I guess you're right."

"Come on then. I'll give you guys the grand tour," he replied, motioning for them to follow him.

"Alright," she agreed. Then turning to look over her shoulder, she called, "Come on, Josh."

He nodded his head and traipsed along behind her, kicking at leaves and picking up a stick that he found lying near the walkway.

"So, which do you want to see first? The buildings or the grounds of the property?" Mr. Martin asked, clapping his hands together and pulling her attention back to him.

She offered him a sheepish smile and answered, "Well, I think Josh would behave better with the outside tour."

"I'd tend to agree with him." Mr. Martin smiled wide. "I've never been much for decorations and furnishings. That's always been my wife's department. No, give me good ole clean air and fresh dirt, and I'm happy."

With that, he turned and lead the tour around the expansive Wild Hearts ranch. There was the pastureland to the west where all the cattle and horses grazed, and then there were the stables and the bunkhouse. As they passed by the corrals, Henry motioned to the fidgety horse inside and stated, "That's another thing we do around here. We rehabilitate horses who've been abused or traumatized in their lives somehow."

Sarah turned her attention to the beautiful white horse, who whinnied in protest at the man trying to approach her.

"Is that really safe?" she asked.

"Oh, don't worry. My men know what they're doing," he responded casually. Then, taking a closer look at the man, he nodded his head and added, "Especially him. He's the best horse whisperer I've got."

She nodded and didn't press him on the issue, even though she did quicken her pace. She didn't want a fight with Josh about horses right now, especially when the horse in question was as fidgety as that horse was.

"Come on, Josh," she called, motioning for him to keep up.

Josh hum-hoed and shoved his hands in his pockets, but he did quicken his pace. She smiled and breathed a prayer of thanks that he was coming along without a fight. That was definitely a win in her book.

"Next on the tour is our vegetable garden," Henry cut into her thoughts. He was beaming as he went on, "It's my pride and joy, and everyone enjoys the fresh goodies it produces."

She smiled at that. "I should probably see it then. If I get the job as the chef around here, I'm going to need plenty of fresh veggies."

He laughed. "Well, what are we waiting for? Let's go."

♥♥♥

"It's alright, Fantasma," Cade stated in a low soothing voice as he approached the skittish Shagya Arabian horse before him. "We're going to be friends, you and me. You'll see."

He kept his hand out as he inched closer, but once again, just as he was about an arm's reach away, the horse threw up her feet and whinnied, darting to the other side of the corral.

He sighed and took off his cattleman hat and ran a hand through his hair, slicking it back before replacing the hat. No one ever said getting a horse to trust you was easy, but it sure did wear on a fella's patience.

"He doesn't seem to like you very much." The young voice from behind him startled him slightly, and he turned around to find a young kid with a mop of dark hair staring at him.

"No, right now, she doesn't trust me at all," he replied, making his way over to this little stranger. "She thinks I'm trying to trick her."

"Are you?" the boy asked.

Cade shook his head. "Nah, I'm just trying to show her that she doesn't have to be afraid anymore."

The little boy considered this before finally puffing out his chest slightly as he stood on the bottom board of the fence to make himself look taller, and he declared, "I'm not afraid of anything."

"Is that so?" Cade smirked at him while tilting his head as he studied the boy. "Does that mean you're one of our newest bull riders?"

"No!" The little boy shook his head and chuckled as if Cade were a dunce. "I'm just a kid."

"Oooohhhhh..." Cade let his head fall back and carried out the word as if he had just realized what the boy was saying was true. "I guess you are." Then, seriously, he focused on the kid and asked, "So, what are you doing out here all by yourself? It can be dangerous around these corrals, Tex."

The little boy laughed. "My name's not Tex. It's Josh, and I'm supposed to be on a tour with Mr. Martin and Aunt Sarah, but I was getting bored. Besides, this looked like way more fun."

Cade peered beyond the boy, but there was no sign of Henry or a woman anywhere. He frowned. What kind of woman would lose her nephew on a ranch like this? Talk about irresponsible!

"So, you just thought you'd go exploring on your own then, huh?" Cade asked, leaning against the corral fence. "Don't you think you should have told your aunt or someone what you were doing?"

Josh's eyes widened, and he shook his head. "I just wanted to watch the horses. Please don't tell on me. I don't like job interviews."

"Job interviews?" Cade repeated, "Is your aunt trying to get a job here?"

Well, that was certainly something he never wanted to see happen. If this was how she treated her nephew, how could she be trusted to handle livestock?

The boy nodded. "Yea, she wants to be a cook," he replied, "She used to be a chef in a fancy restaurant, but she said she wanted to spend more time with me because I was getting into a lot of trouble at school. So, now we've got to move..." Josh shrugged. "I wasn't happy about it at first, but I like this ranch. So, I think I'm okay with it now."

"Oh, really?" Cade smiled at that. "So, you want to be a ranch hand some day?"

Josh nodded his head excitedly. "If it means I get to work with horses, I would! I love horses!"

With that, Cade got an idea, and he clapped his hands together. "Well, if you like horses, I think I have a job just for you."

"Really?!" Josh's eyes were as huge as saucers now. "What is it?"

"Well, it's a pretty difficult job, and we don't let just anyone do it..."

"What is it!?" Josh exclaimed.

"Brushing down a horse," Cade stated quickly.

A huge smile burst across Josh's face. "So, I'd actually get to touch a horse!" he nearly shouted, "I'm in!"

Cade smiled to himself as he ducked through the fence and ruffled the boy's hair. "Alright then. Let's go."

"Well, I think I've bored you enough with the outside." Henry winked at her in a teasing way. "How about we head on into the mess hall where you'll be spending most of your time? I mean, if you agree to take the job, that is..."

She faltered slightly. "You mean—I've got it?" she asked in shock. They hadn't even talked about the job yet in this interview. He had just seemed content to show her his garden and chickens and cows...

He smiled wide at her. "Of course! I mean, to be honest, you're extremely qualified... perhaps, even overqualified for this job. You made quite the name for yourself at that fancy restaurant where you used to work. What was it called? The Kalander?"

"The Kalanchow," she informed him.

"That's right!" he replied with a nod, "The Kalanchow. My wife and I stopped there last year when we were nearby on business, and I must say your cooking lived up to all the hype!"

"Well, I had a good team too," she reminded him.

He smiled at that. "Yea, but without a great leader at the helm, it wouldn't have been so good. Besides, your coming here is quite the blessing for us too, even though I can't pay you what that restaurant could."

"That's alright," she stated quickly, "I can't do the long hours at the restaurant anymore, not with Josh now.

I need flexibility, and I'm willing to sacrifice some cash for that."

"That's what I like about you. You know what you want, and you're going after it. Well, if you want the job, I can offer you the salary we discussed over the phone, plus free room and board and meals too."

"That sounds wonderful! You don't know how long I've been searching for a job like this!" she exclaimed, her body relaxing as relief flooded through her. "I was beginning to think I would never find a new job! And Josh and I were getting so tired of traveling and looking for one. You can't even imagine!" She smiled to herself as she once again prayed a silent thank you to the Lord. They were going to be okay.

She turned around to ask Josh what he thought, but what she saw—or rather didn't see—caused her stomach to drop as an icy pit began to form in her chest. It crept all throughout her body, and her heart began to race. She rushed to the corner of the nearby chicken coop and looked behind it, but there was no sign of him.

"Josh!" she shouted, looking around her frantically. When had he wondered off? How had she not noticed?

Henry walked over to her and placed a hand on her shoulder. "Don't worry. He's just probably looking at the animals somewhere nearby. We'll find him. We just have to retrace our steps..."

Just then, before he could say anymore, his phone began to ring, and he answered it, holding up one finger towards her. She supposed it was an effort to tell her he wouldn't be long, but she wanted to scream. Josh was gone. What was she going to do?!

She shook her head as Henry turned around talking into his phone, but his words repeated themselves in her mind. Don't worry. She found that one was easier said than done. Worry had always been something she struggled with, even as a child, but in light of recent events, it was just getting worse. She rubbed her upper arms to try and warm herself up. She could feel the shakes beginning, and she inhaled deeply to calm herself. The key was to breathe. She kept telling herself this over and over again. She prayed the panic attack would stop before it got beyond her control. She needed to find Josh. She needed to be there for him. She couldn't panic now. He was counting on her. In and out, she repeated this over and over, praying it would pass. She took in deep breaths and let them out. She couldn't believe she had let something like this happen! She wasn't fit to be a mother! She couldn't even take care of one child! In and out...

Henry ended his call and clapped his hands together. "Well, good news! That was one of my men. He's got Josh with him."

"He does?!" She could feel the relief reverberate through her body like a shock wave. She was still shaking but not as bad now. "Where is he? I need to see him!"

Henry smiled wide. "Come on. I'll lead the way. See? I told you there was nothing to fret over."

She inhaled deeply once again, and this time when she exhaled, she breathed a prayer of thanks to God that Josh was safe and sound with...

"Cade!" she exclaimed as she and Henry walked into the horse stable near where she had seen the skittish but beautiful white horse before.

He turned around to face her, his face a mix of surprise and disappointment. She frowned. How could he still look the same after all these years?! Well, she took in his full appearance quickly and realized he wasn't exactly the same. He had grown up. All his time in the rodeo circuit had made him muscular, not that he had showy muscles but rather the kind you get from hard work. His dark black hair was styled in the same way he had always kept it, short all over with the bangs spiked up, and his grey eyes were as piercing as ever. She couldn't help but admit that he was still handsome after all these years. The rodeo hadn't changed that...In fact, it might have improved him some. She couldn't believe herself! She shook her head, trying to focus her thoughts on the matter at hand. How could she even remotely be thinking of him in that way?! Force of habit probably. She had been in love with him once. Why? She couldn't even remember. All she could think of was the way it had ended. She would never forget that. That memory would always be with her.

"Sarah." He said her name like it pained him, and he nodded in her direction. "I think you lost something." He sidestepped so she could see Josh as he worked, brushing down a horse with a curry comb. She was about to call Josh's name when she saw the huge smile on his face. She hadn't seen him smile like that since...She blinked...Since the accident.

She frowned. She had thought this time it would work out. That this job would be the one, but obviously not. If Cade worked here, there was no way she could.

Not after what he had done. The only thing she hated was that she was going to have to disappoint Josh. He looked like he was loving it here. He would hate her for taking him away from this place and heading out on the road again in search of the next one, but how could she take a job here now? No, she couldn't work with Cade. It was out of the question.

"Wait, you two know each other?" Henry asked. "How come I didn't know that?"

Cade shrugged. "We knew each other a long time ago. It's ancient history now."

She crossed her arms, glaring at him. A long time ago....Ancient history, huh? She frowned. Well, if he was going to pretend like this didn't bother him, then she could do that too. She wasn't the same girl she had been all those years ago. She could show him that he meant nothing to her now too.

"So, you're wanting to work here, huh?" he asked.

"I had considered it..." she admitted curtly.

She stopped herself short of saying what she really wanted to say. That there was no way on God's green earth that she would ever—EVER!— be caught working on the same ranch as Cade Jacobs.

CHAPTER TWO

C ade Jacobs couldn't believe that Sarah Makenna was this little kid's absent and lax aunt. He shook his head. She had been nothing like that in high school. She was always the girl with all the answers, who knew exactly where she was going and what she wanted. She had also been the person that had made it clear that she wanted nothing to do with him all those years ago...That he didn't fit into her perfect life image. He grated his teeth. He would never have guessed that she would do something like lose a child on a ranch like this though. He crossed his arms. Well, people could change over the years, and ten years was a long time. Perhaps, she wasn't the same as he remembered. He frowned as memories began to flood his mind again unbidden. He had thought he had been able to put his past behind him but, being confronted with it so suddenly, had certainly proved just how wrong he was.

He eyed her subtly and realized that she really hadn't changed all that much over the years. She'd let her hair grow out, and it suited her. She was still sleek and stylish. Her cheeks didn't hold that same glow that they used to years ago, and she wasn't as tan as she once was. He figured working somewhere other than a ranch could do that to a person. He shook his head, wondering how she could look the same and yet different at the same time. He guessed that the fact that she looked like something out of his memories was what had him feeling so mixed up. He just hadn't been ready to face his past. That's why he was having so much trouble focusing on anything other than her at the moment. He was sure that was the reason. It had to be. He had wanted nothing to do with her after she'd dumped him, and that's how he still felt. He was not going back to that ever!

"Well, what a coincidence!" Henry stated, pulling Cade back into reality, "Imagine that. You two meeting here after all these years."

Cade nodded. "Yea, imagine." Then, motioning towards the boy, he added, "Well, since you've found him, you'll probably want to be on your way, right?"

25

She opened her mouth to argue, but before she could say anything, Henry began to laugh, slapping Cade on the arm.

"Oh, Cade, always the jokester! Don't pay any attention to him," Henry stated, though he sounded a bit unsure of himself. He eyed the two of them before continuing, "Since you're our new cook, I'm sure you'll get used to Cade's teasing in no time."

"New cook?" Cade's eyes widened. "You want to be the cook?!"

What had happened to all her grand dreams? She'd never once talked about being a cook. Things really had changed over the years.

She frowned slightly and looked away from Cade for the first time since she'd recognized him, turning her attention to Henry, and she stated, "About that, Henry, I think I might need some time before I commit to anything."

"What?! Why?" Henry exclaimed, shock washing over his face, "I thought we had it all settled."

"Well, some things have come up..."

At that, her glare locked once more on Cade, and he just smirked defiantly at her. She could try to blame this on him, but this was all her. She was running away just because she wasn't getting her way like she always did.

"And I'm just not sure this is the right place for Josh and I."

"What?!" Josh nearly shouted as he rushed over to them, "But I like it here. There're horses."

"There'll be horses other places too," Sarah quickly stated.

Henry shook his head. "Alright, I'm not really sure what's happening here, but I know how to get to the bottom of it," he declared, "How about y'all join me and my wife for supper tonight? We can clear all of this up then. Emmie might be retiring as our cook, but my wife's still the best around. What do y'all say?"

"No thanks, Henry," Cade stated, shaking his head. He had had enough of Miss Makenna to last him a lifetime. "I think I'll pass, but tell Emmie I said hi."

"Oh, come on, Cade," Henry urged him, but Cade shook his head.

"I've got work to do," he explained, "Maybe some other time."

"Well, Sarah, surely you'll come," Henry pressed, "Maybe then we can discuss the cook position better?" Then, when Sarah hesitated, he quickly added, "Did I mention my wife's cooking her famous fried chicken and mashed potatoes with her homemade gravy? Plus, green beans picked fresh from our garden and rolls too!"

"Please, Aunt Sarah," Josh begged, "I don't want to eat at the hotel again!"

Sarah sighed, wrapping an arm protectively around Josh's shoulders, and she nodded. "I suppose we can stay for supper." Then, glaring once more at Cade, she added, "I guess it wouldn't hurt."

"Excellent, come on, you two! It should almost be time to eat now," Henry called with a wave of his hand, and Sarah and Josh started to follow him out of the barn.

Cade shook his head and turned back towards the horse Josh had been brushing down. He patted her on the nose and picked up the brush to finish the job, but just then, he realized he wasn't alone. He looked over to see Josh, staring up at him with big eyes.

"Aren't you coming to eat too?" Josh asked.

Cade smiled at him but shook his head, crossing his arms and leaning against the stall door. "Nah, not this time, kid. I'm not hungry. Plus, I've got a bunch of work around here to do."

"Oh..." Josh's face fell, and he sighed.

"Josh, come on now," Sarah called from the entrance to the stable, "You don't want to bother Cade. Let's go."

"I'm not bothering him!" Josh protested, "Am I?"

Cade laughed and shook his head. "Nope."

"Good!" Josh smiled proudly. "Then, I think I had better stay and help you finish your work so you can come eat too!"

"Josh..." Sarah stressed the word, but the little boy didn't budge.

"I think you'd better go with your aunt," Cade replied, motioning with his head towards Sarah, "There'll be plenty of time for you to help with the horses later if your aunt chooses to work here."

"You mean it?!" Josh exclaimed, his eyes wide.

Cade chuckled and nodded his head. "Sure do. Haven't you ever heard that a rancher's job is never done?"

Josh smiled a toothy grin, but just then, Sarah called to him again, causing his shoulders to slump.

"I'm coming," he stated as he hurried over to her. Then, turning, he waved at Cade calling out "Bye!" as he did. Cade smiled and waved back. Josh reminded him of Sarah before the accident ten years ago. She had been so

29

carefree then, and she had loved horses so much! She was a cowgirl through and through. Then, after the accident...everything had changed.

Sarah placed a hand on Josh's back to make sure he didn't wander off again as they followed Henry, but even as she left the barn, Cade couldn't get her out of his mind. Why was she here? Out of all the ranches in the world, why had she had to choose this one?! It just didn't make sense!

A low rumble of thunder echoed nearby in the distance, and he frowned as he realized the wind had picked up. They were most likely in for another pop up spring storm. He needed to get things put up around the barns and get the horses ready for it too before it hit.

He blew out a breath and shook his head as he started to head back to work, but try as he might, he couldn't get that fiery blonde or her kid nephew out of his mind. Would Sarah actually take the job here? Would he and Sarah Makenna actually be working together again? He frowned. There was no way....He just couldn't do that. Not again. Not after everything. But maybe he'd get lucky, and she'd turn the job down now. He turned his eyes heavenward and prayed a little prayer that she'd do just that before sticking a piece of straw in his mouth. He glanced once more up at the gray clouds rolling in as he headed outside and started working. He just hoped she didn't stick around here. The last thing he needed was some high and mighty princess hanging around, dictating what he could and couldn't do with his life again...

Sarah's mind was racing as she and Josh followed Henry towards his house. At first, she had felt furious with Cade. Who did he think he was behaving like that?! She couldn't believe after all these years that that was all he'd had to say to her! At least, he could have apologized for running off to the rodeo and abandoning her ten years ago! After that though, worry would begin to nag at her. Josh seemed fascinated by Cade. It was just because he was a cowboy, and Josh was really into trying to be one right now, right? That was it, she consoled herself, but still the thought that it could be something more needled at her. Josh was so much like Cade at times. She feared those two being around each other would expose things better left buried, and she couldn't risk that. No, the sooner she got Josh away from Cade the better. She had worked too long and too hard to bury the past, and her reasons for doing so were still the same.

She blew out a breath. If she were honest with herself, just seeing Cade again had rattled her. Just seeing him again here...in person...after all these years... She hadn't been prepared for all the emotions it would stir up. She had thought she had buried all of that history in the past, but then, glancing at Josh, she frowned. Apparently, she hadn't.

She shook her head and turned her eyes heavenward. Why, God? Why did it have to be him? Why did he have to work here? There are so many kids I went to school with that I never have seen again. Why couldn't Cade Jacobs have been one of them? This is the last thing I need right now!

"That's why the ranch is so large now," Mr. Martin's talking pulled her out of her prayer and back into the here and now, "It's funny how God works all things out, isn't it?"

She blinked as she tried to piece together what he was talking about, but to be honest, she had gotten so lost in her own thoughts, she had not been listening to a word. She sighed, realizing she was just going to have to admit her mistake.

"I'm sorry. What were you saying?" she asked.

Henry laughed and shook his head. "If I'm boring you, just tell me. I have a tendency to talk for hours unless someone stops me."

"Oh, it's not that!" she quickly protested, "I was just lost in thought. It's been a long day."

"Already?" He winked at her, and she realized he was teasing her.

Her shoulders relaxed, and she offered him a smile. However, she wasn't about to tell him the truth about what she had been thinking about. Instead, she settled for telling him something else. "Yea, I'm new to this whole parenting thing, and it really wears you out."

"You're telling me?" He laughed, "I raised four boys myself and two girls. I was plumb exhausted most of my life, but I've loved every minute of it."

"Oh, wow, you really did have your hands full!" she exclaimed.

He nodded. "But they were all good kids. Like Josh here, they always loved helping with the horses. They still come back to the ranch from time to time."

Speaking of Josh, she turned to look down at him. She had kept her hand on his back to make sure he didn't wander off this time. He was being surprisingly quiet, and she wondered what had him so deep in thought. So, she nudged him slightly.

"Whatcha' thinking about, Josh?" she asked him.

"Oh, just the horses," Josh replied, "I think I could be a real good cowboy if we stayed here."

"A really good cowboy," she corrected his grammar.

"Whatever," he scoffed. Then, turning to look up at her with big eyes, he asked, "Why can't we stay here, Aunt Sarah?"

"I haven't made up my mind, Josh. It's a big decision, and there's a lot to consider," she informed him.

"But you said this morning that you really wanted this job!" Josh protested, "What happened?!"

Sarah was at a loss for words. How could she explain to him what seeing Cade here had done to her plans? There was no way he would understand what she was thinking.

"Sometimes, Son, certain things happen, and our plans don't work out the way we think they will," Henry jumped in, "When that happens, we have a choice to make. Do we ride the wave no matter how choppy or do we bail out? I think that's what your aunt's facing right now."

"What's he talking about?" Josh asked.

She sighed. Why did kids have to ask so many questions?

"I'll explain it to you later," she replied, nudging him to keep moving. Just then, she felt a rush of wind whip her hair around, and she was struck by its suddenness.

"We'd better hurry inside," Henry called back to them, "There's a storm coming on fast. You can feel it in the air."

Sarah looked around her, and she frowned at the dark storm clouds rolling in. He was right. A storm was coming. How had she not noticed it before now? A raindrop hit her on the cheek, and she quickened her pace. She'd have time to wonder about that when she was inside where it would be nice and dry.

Once the storm hit, it took no time at all before it turned into a powerful thunderstorm, and Cade was glad he had already put the horses up, especially Fantasma. She hated storms more than the rest. Even now, she bucked and kicked at her stall, protesting every loud crash of thunder. He frowned and took off his hat, running a hand through his damp hair. She would calm down as soon as the storm was over. Another loud crash, and the sky lit up with a flash of lightning. A sudden gust of wind yanked open one of the barn doors, causing Fantasma to whinny in terror. He shook his head, wondering how that had happened. He'd probably failed to latch it properly when he'd brought in...His mind trailed off as he reached for the door only to catch sight of a lightning bolt striking a tree over near the drive, splitting it in two instantly. The massive tree fell over the drive with a crash, and Cade's shoulders slumped. That was going to be a mess to clean up tomorrow. Then, he caught sight of Sarah's car still parked in the visitor's section, and his lips formed a thin line. He was going to have to go to the Martins' and tell her she wasn't getting out of here tonight. He cringed. That wasn't something he wanted to do, but it couldn't be helped. He may not like who she had grown up to be, but that didn't mean he wanted her to get soaked and brave this storm for nothing. He shook his head as the horses behind him cried out again. He needed to stop thinking and get this door closed. So, with that thought in mind, he replaced his hat on his head and pulled up his coat collar around his neck. Shutting and latching the door behind him, he hurriedly made his way up to the main house where Sarah was still having dinner with the Martins. The rain was coming down in thick sheets that stung his face, and the wind whipped around him, threatening to make him lose his balance on the slippery ground around him. He shielded his eyes and stayed focused on the porch light of the Martins' place, one heavy footstep after the other. He shook his head. This had grown into some storm. Finally, he climbed up onto the porch, and the roof gave him a bit of a reprieve from the rain. He knocked on the door before taking off his hat and shaking the water off of it.

Almost immediately, the door opened, and Henry stood there.

"Cade?" he asked in surprise at the sight of him. "Change your mind?"

He shook his head. "No, I just came to let you and Miss Makenna know that one of the old oaks came down over the drive."

"Oh, dear," Emmie declared as she hurried over to her husband, "No one was hurt, were they?"

"No, Ma'am, but the drive is completely blocked."

"Oh-no!" Sarah exclaimed from inside, "How are we going to get back to our hotel?"

"Well, you'll just have to stay here of course!" Mrs. Martin declared as she turned to face the two of them at the table, "You'll stay in the cabin. It's yours anyway if you take the job. It just hasn't been cleaned yet I'm afraid."

Sarah relaxed in her chair and offered Mrs. Martin a smile. "It's fine. I'm sure. Thank you! We really appreciate that."

His message delivered, Cade turned to leave, but Emmie caught his arm before he could get away.

"Cade Jacobs, you get in here this instant and dry off. You're soaked to the bone," she ordered in her motherly tone. He gave her a lopsided smile as he took a step backwards.

"That's alright, Emmie," he offered, "I'm fine."

"Cade..." she hissed his name, "Don't you backtalk me. Now, get in here."

His shoulders slumped slightly. So much for his quick get away. Mrs. Martin had a way about her that made it nearly impossible for him to say no to her for long. Perhaps, it was because she sort of reminded him of his mom...At least what he could remember of her.

"You win." He smirked at her as he stepped inside the door, and Henry laughed, slapping him on the back and causing rainwater from his jacket to fly everywhere as he did.

"I knew you couldn't resist Emmie's fried chicken!" Henry exclaimed.

Cade shook his head, raising up his hands quickly. "I don't want to impose on your supper. I'll just dry off in the other room," he replied, purposefully keeping his gaze fixed on Emmie and Henry, and not on the woman sitting at the table behind him. She looked pretty with the candlelight warming her cheeks and highlighting her dusty blonde hair. He frowned, forcing those thoughts aside. She was more trouble than she was worth. He had learned that years ago, and it was a lesson that had left its scars on his heart. He wasn't about to forget it just because of a little candlelight.

"Nonsense, you can dry off in here and fill your stomach while you're at it," Emmie declared, "You haven't eaten your supper yet, have you?"

He grimaced. He couldn't lie to her, but he had a feeling that was the only way he was going to get out of this awkward dinner.

"I thought so," she stated, nodding her head triumphantly. "Now, take off your wet things and hang 'em up over there. Then, you can take a seat by the fireplace. You'll be dry in no time."

He sighed, and obediently, he shrugged off his coat and hung it up with his hat. He slid onto the bench that ran alongside the table and in front of the fireplace. Unfortunately, that also put him right across from Sarah, and by the way she was staring anywhere but in his direction, he got the feeling that she was no happier about this than he was. Emmie finished dishing up his heaping plate and set it in front of him.

"There!" She smiled happily as she took her seat at the end of the table. "Now, you can just relax and let the storm pass us by." Then, turning to Sarah, she added, "Plus, it'll give you a chance to get to know Sarah and her nephew. Sarah's interested in being our new cook."

"So, I've heard," he stated simply with a quick look between Emmie and Sarah.

"Oh?" Emmie asked, looking surprised by his tone.

Sarah nodded. "Cade and I've met. Actually..." Her tone changed to an upbeat but sarcastic one as she continued, "We used to date, but that's ancient history now."

She shot him a defiant look, and it wasn't lost on him that she had used his own wording. Before he could contemplate that any farther though, Emmie spoke up.

"Oh, I see," she stated, with a contemplative nod, "Now, things are beginning to make sense."

He cringed. He didn't need Emmie digging into his past. She was already always trying to set him up with the young ladies that came to work here. He didn't need her meddling in this area of his life too.

"Cade taught me how to brush horses today!" Josh announced happily before shoving a spoonful of potatoes into his mouth.

"He did?" Emmie smiled wide, giving both Josh and Cade an approving look, but Cade just shrank down slightly in his seat, wondering why he had come here again. This was the last thing he had wanted to do today especially with Sarah sitting across from him and giving him that death glare of hers.

"Yep, and since we're going to be living here now, he's going to teach me how to ride horses too!" Josh declared triumphantly.

Cade's eyes widened as his gaze shot to the child's, and Sarah whipped around to face him, her eyes blazing at Cade. He shook his head. Not that he cared what Sarah thought of him, but this time it wasn't his fault. He opened his mouth to say just that, but the words died in his throat at the sight of the boy's hopeful eyes. Gone was the forlorn little boy he had met earlier. He was happy, full of hope and excited about the future. He couldn't take that away from him.

"Well, I'm sure we can find you a nice pony to ride," Emmie added, nodding her head, but her eyes studied Sarah and Cade carefully.

"Josh, we're not even sure if we're going to be living here, remember?" Sarah stressed to her nephew as she finally wrenched her fiery gaze away from Cade and instead turned her focus on Josh. "And even if I did take this job, you know I don't want you riding horses." Her words were polite, but they were full of controlled emotion. She was furious. She was just trying really hard not to show it. Cade smirked at that. Same old Sarah.

Cade grabbed a spoonful of potatoes, but before he ate them, he said, "What's wrong with the kid riding horses? I thought you just hated the rodeo life. What you got against horses now?"

"I do hate the rodeo and what it does to people. I would have thought you would agree with me now after your last accident." Her words were laced with venom, and they hit their mark, wiping the smirk right off his face.

He frowned. How had she known about his accident? Had she been following his career all these years?

"Besides," Sarah continued before he was able to get his racing mind to form a coherent response, "Josh's too little to ride horses."

"You're kidding?!" Cade nearly laughed at that. "How old were you when your dad put you on your first horse? Like two?"

Her face reddened, and she waved a hand dismissively at him while her gaze darted away from his. "That's different."

"How so?" he challenged, leaning forward and relishing finally being able to make her squirm a bit.

Poor Emmie and Henry looked confused by all of this, but he wasn't about to back down now.

She looked away and crossed her arms. "It just is, okay? He's too young, and that's final."

"But you said that I coul—" Josh started with pleading eyes staring up at her.

"I never said that," she corrected him, "I said maybe when you were older."

"But I am older!" Josh protested.

Henry laughed at that, and Sarah sighed. "Only by a few hours. That isn't enough. When, you're big enough, then you can—"

"I'm big enough now!" Josh argued. Then, turning to Cade with expectant eyes, he asked, "Aren't I?"

Cade opened his mouth, but he wasn't sure what words he wanted to come out.

"Well, there will be plenty of time to decide about horse riding lessons later," Emmie jumped in, saving him from having to say anything.

Henry took the hint and cleared his throat before shoveling another forkful of green beans into his mouth. "You sure out did yourself on the grub, Honey!"

"Yes, it's delicious," Sarah agreed, in a much quieter tone now.

"It is really good." Cade nodded, awkwardly eating another spoonful.

"I still think I'm big enough to ride horses," Josh grumbled, slumping down in his seat.

"Josh," Sarah whispered sternly, "Eat your food."

He crossed his arms, just staring at his plate, and her shoulders slumped in defeat. Cade sighed, not knowing whether he was crazy or not for what he was about to do.

"You know, kid," Cade stated, his gaze on the little boy and purposefully avoiding Sarah, "Cowboys have to eat lots of food to grow big and strong that way they can ride and take care of the horses."

"Really?!" Josh asked, his eyes widening.

Cade nodded his head, and when he turned his gaze away, he noticed Sarah sitting there looking astonished at him. He smiled at her before ducking his gaze down quickly. Just because they didn't see eye to eye on anything anymore didn't mean he couldn't help her out if he wanted to.

Immediately, Josh picked up his fork and started shoveling food into his mouth so fast Cade was afraid he was going to choke. At the sight of him eating, Sarah's demeanor softened slightly, but she still seemed to avoid looking at him throughout the rest of the supper.

"Whoa, slow down there, buckaroo," Henry chuckled, "Those horses'll still be there when you get done."

45

Josh smiled and laughed turning to face Henry. "Sorry."

And with that, he started to eat at a normal pace. Cade smiled as he watched the kid. He was the spitting image of Sarah's dad when he was that age. Cade had been around their place enough to see tons of family photos over the years, but that thought gave him pause. He wondered how she felt about the likeness. She was probably grateful for it, but then again, it must be painful, especially since he seemed to have that same love for horses as his granddaddy. Cade frowned. What did it matter to him? She wasn't a part of his life anymore. It shouldn't matter what would upset her or not. He took another bite of his fried chicken. But for some weird reason, he couldn't get the thought of her crying over her dad's accident ten years ago out of his mind. It had been so sudden, and it had devastated the entire family. He blinked his eyes as he snuck a look over at her. He wondered if things could have been different between them had they handle the aftermath of that accident differently. What if they had talked it out? Let each other know what they were feeling instead of acting impulsively on emotion...She looked over at him and frowned. Immediately, he dropped his gaze to the chicken and served himself another helping. He once again stole a look at her. She was studying him now, but when she saw his gaze, she immediately looked away. No, things wouldn't have ended up differently, he reminded himself. The two of them had wanted different things. They had been destined to fall apart. They had just figured it out during a rather hard time. He leaned back against his chair, staring at his food. The sooner he accepted that the better. He just hoped he could remember it even if she did start working here...

CHAPTER THREE

The next morning, Sarah stepped out of her cabin and stretched, inhaling the fresh air and enjoying the birds' morning songs. The cabin was small, but it was big enough for Josh and her with its two bedrooms, full bath, kitchenette, and an open concept living room. She blew on the top of her cup of tea as steam rose up in the chilly morning air. She could get used to this. She smiled contentedly.

Just then, however, she saw Cade walking from the bunkhouse towards the barn, all decked out in his work clothes. From the red and black flannel he wore to the thick gloves and cowboy boots, he looked like he was ready to mend fences or wrangle cattle or something else out of an old western. She frowned at the sight of him, her grip tightening on her mug. Reality hit her once more, and she reminded herself that this was only temporary. No matter how wonderful this place may seem, there was no way she could work here with him. Seeing him brought up memories, too many memories, and then there was Josh...She shook her head before taking a sip of tea. Josh seemed awestruck by him. There was something about Cade that Josh seemed to just get, and that concerned her. She couldn't risk the truth about Josh slipping out. That's why she needed to get him out of here before any real damage could be done. Josh was hers now, and she was not about to do anything to risk losing him again.

A wave of sadness washed over her as she was once again reminded of how much she missed her sister. Kelsie had always been the best big sister a girl could ever hope for, and when Sarah had approached her with the news that she was going to have a baby and she didn't know what to do, Kelsie had hatched a scheme to keep everyone happy. She would raise Josh like he was her son because Kelsie and her husband hadn't been able to have any children of their own. Then, Sarah would still be able to see her baby, but she wouldn't be a single mom or have to tell Cade the news, which would forever have formed a chain between her and him, whether they liked it or not. So, they had went away together on a long trip, and by the end of it, Kelsie had adopted Josh and told everyone that he was her and her husband's son. Sarah had thought this to be the best arrangement at the time because she was single and only had a part-time job. What kind of life could she have given Josh then? So, she had gone along with her sister's plan, but Sarah had never dreamed of how hard it would be to see her son and not be able to claim him. Their plan had seemed so simple, so easy. Little did she know how much it would kill her day by day. Hearing him call someone else Momma broke her heart a little at a time, and even now that he was finally with her, he still only viewed her as his aunt. He resented her because she wasn't his mom. She had just been trying to protect him and do what was best for him, but now, she wondered if they had made a terrible mistake. She frowned, subtly swiping away the tears from her eyes. It had been so much easier to run from the pain when her sister was the one taking care of him, but now they were gone. Now, she was left to pay the full punishment of her sin all alone. She straightened her shoulders. That may be, but she was still going to do her best for Josh, not only for her sister but also for herself.

She finished the last swig of her tea as Cade disappeared from view, and she shook her head. It was time to go, and with that, she headed inside to get Josh and do just that.

Cade mounted his horse, Brego, and headed for the parking lot. That big oak was going to be quite the chore to get rid of, but he knew it needed to be done. After all, the sooner he got rid of it the sooner Sarah could leave and get out of his life again.

It wasn't that long of a ride from the barn to the visitor parking lot, but he had a feeling he would need Brego's help to remove the tree piece by piece. Once they arrived at the parking lot, Cade got his first look at the job before him, and he let out a low whistle. Yea, that tree had been one massive oak!

"Hey there, Mr. Cade!" Matt, one of the young ranch hands, called out with a wave as he approached on foot, lugging a chainsaw with him as if it were going to yank him down to the ground.

Cade waved as he slid down off his black Arabian horse, and he offered Brego a sugar cube stating, "Good boy, Brego."

His horse gratefully accepted it, and Cade stroked his snout, as he tried to hide the smirk that threatened to emerge at the sight of Matt. The kid was thin and scrawny. There wasn't a lick of muscles on him yet, and Cade had no doubt that that chainsaw was, in fact, trying to pull him down to the ground.

"I got the chainsaw!"

Cade nodded. "So, I see."

"Here you go," Matt declared, holding the chainsaw out to him.

Cade took it along with some safety glasses that Matt had brought along too.

"Don't you want to use it?" Cade asked, motioning to the chainsaw.

"Ummm...I don't know how," Matt admitted, shifting on his feet uncomfortably.

Cade felt sorry for the kid. He was a city slicker through and through, and all this country living was brand new to him. Still, his parents had insisted he work here for the season. They had thought it would help him grow, and Cade believed they were right. The country, in his opinion, was the best place to grow and learn about yourself. It was a lot of hard work, but it was so worth it.

He loved it. He almost felt sorry for those city slickers who would never know what they were missing.

"Alright then. I'll start, but I want you to watch me," Cade informed him, "I'm going to get you going. That way you can take over, and you'll know how to do it the next time around."

"O—okay. If you say so." Matt nodded nervously as he put on his safety glasses.

So, with that settled, Cade set to work chopping up bits of the tree and instructing Matt on what he was doing at the same time. It was a slow process, but it was a good opportunity for Matt. If he learned how to handle this right here and now, it would save Cade trouble farther down the line.

When they were almost finished, he handed the saw over to Matt and stated, "It's all yours, buddy."

Matt hesitated. "Are you sure I'm ready?"

"You can do it," Cade declared, handing it to him, and reluctantly, Matt took it from him and turned to face what was left of the tree. Swallowing hard, he turned the chainsaw on and started to cut the tree.

Just then, Josh walked up behind Cade and tugged on his flannel. Cade whipped around to find the little boy there, and he immediately stooped down to his level.

"You shouldn't be here," he stated in a voice louder than the chainsaw, "It's too dangerous."

"But I had to talk to you," the little boy protested.

Cade's shoulders slumped slightly, and he glanced over his shoulder at Matt, who appeared fine.

Cade nodded his head. "Alright, come over here where we can talk," he replied.

The little guy followed obediently, and once they were farther away from the chainsaw, Cade asked him, "Okay, what was it you needed to talk with me about?"

"Aunt Sarah says I can't ride horses," he informed him, and Cade inwardly cringed. This was not something he wanted to discuss, but the little boy seemed adamant. "But I want to ride so badly. Why can't I?"

"Well, if your aunt said..."

"She's not my mom," Josh grumbled, crossing his arms, "Why does she get to tell me what to do?"

"Come on," Cade tried to cheer him up, "I'm sure she's just trying to do what she thinks is right."

"But it's not fair! I want to be a cowboy too!" Josh protested.

"Well, sometimes we have to listen to others even when—"

"Is that your horse?" Josh exclaimed, rushing over to Brego.

Cade nodded, following behind him. "Yea, his name is Brego."

"Brego—That's cool. Where'd you get it?" Josh asked.

"From a book trilogy I read in high school," Cade replied.

Josh nodded, but he was no longer listening. He was stroking the horse's nuzzle gently as if he were afraid Brego might vanish suddenly. Cade smiled at him, wishing Sarah could see Josh like this. If she did, he had a feeling she might just change her mind about her no horses policy.

Just then, Matt must have gotten the chainsaw too close to the ground and hit a stone or something because whatever it was shot off from where he was working, hitting Brego in the rear. Instinctively, the horse cried out in pain and reared up, his front legs kicking in the process. Cade didn't even hesitate to think. He lunged over, grabbing Josh and pulling him away from the horse to protect him. In the process, Brego accidentally kicked Cade in the arm, and Cade had to bite his lower lip to keep from crying out. Better for the kid not to know he had gotten hurt. He spun around in a swift motion, leaving him standing with his back to Brego and Josh in his arms. By now, Brego had calmed himself down, but the horse shifted over trying to move farther away from the area with the chainsaw.

Matt turned around to look at them in shock, and Cade motioned for him to turn off the chainsaw. Immediately, Matt did so with a look of concern on his face.

"What were you thinking?!" Sarah Makenna's shout could clearly be heard now, and Cade closed his eyes. When he had wished she could see Josh and Brego together, that had not been what he'd meant.

She stormed up to him as Cade put Josh down, and she jammed her finger into his chest.

"You just won't be satisfied until he's hurt too! Will you!?"

"Whoa," Cade exclaimed, raising up his hands in surrender and grimacing slightly at the pain in his one arm, but it wasn't anything he wasn't already used too. The rodeo had taught him how to handle pain a long time ago. "Hang on a second. You can't possibly think that this was my fault."

She crossed her arms over her chest and tapped her foot impatiently. "And who's fault would it be then?" She glared at him, daring him to argue.

Cade opened his mouth to answer, but Josh quickly stepped forward, saying, "I was just waiting for you, Aunt Sarah, and while I was, I stopped to talk with Cade. Then, when I saw his horse, I just had to see him! Cade told me it was dangerous, but I wanted to stay. It's not his fault, Aunt Sarah. It's mine!"

"Well, actually, Ma'am, it was my fault," Matt volunteered, stepping forward slightly before stopping himself, "Cade warned me to keep the chainsaw away from the ground, but I made a mistake and misjudged the distance."

Cade shook his head and waved Matt off. "It's okay, Matt. It was an accident."

"It's okay!" She whirled around to face Cade once again, her eyes blazing. "That horse could have trampled Josh, but to you, it's okay?!"

Cade sighed, looking up at the sky. God needed to give him some of His patience right about now, because he was growing tired of always having to explain himself.

"You know that's not what I meant, Sarah," he replied, his shoulders slumping.

She shook her head and laughed, not a ha ha that's funny type of laugh, but rather a "I can't believe this is happening" type of laugh.

"Why out of all the ranches in all the country did you have to work here?!" she snapped, "God knows I don't need this right now!"

"Sarah, come on. It was an accident," Cade offered softly, like he was talking to a wild mustang.

"And I'm fine, Aunt Sarah," Josh piped in, "Honest."

"A horse nearly trampled you!" she exclaimed.

"I know what you saw looked kind of bad," Cade admitted, "But you're overreacting."

"Overreacting?!" She shook her head. "Why am I even bothering talking to you? I'd get better results talking to a rock than you! I should've learned my lesson years ago!" She grabbed Josh by his arm and snapped, "Come on, Josh. Let's go!"

"But wait, Aunt Sarah," Josh protested, "I want to say goodbye to—"

"Now, Josh," she ordered, pulling him after her.

Josh waved his hand limply at Cade, his eyes sad.
"Bye," he called, "Sorry I got you in trouble."

"Don't worry about it, Kid." Cade winked at him.
"I can take care of myself."

Sarah shot him a look over her shoulder as she
unlocked her CRV and motioned for Josh to get inside.
Cade's smile vanished as he watched her. Why did she
hate him so much? Wasn't she the one who had dumped
him? He should be the one full of hate, not her. He blew
out a breath and hung his head.

"I'm sorry, Cade," Matt quickly offered, rushing
up to him, "I didn't mean to do that."

"It wasn't your fault, Matt. It was an accident. It
could have happened to anybody," Cade replied, placing
his good hand on Matt's shoulder before turning his
attention to Brego. He dragged his hand over his horse's
body to calm him before checking his hindquarters for
any injury. Luckily, the stone must have just grazed him,
bouncing off without leaving a mark. Cade's shoulders
relaxed at that. Brego then jostled the back of Cade's
head, tipping his hat down over his eyes, and Cade
laughed, turning around to face his horse. He stroked his
nose and stated, "It's alright. I forgive you too."

"Boy, she sure was mad," Matt whistled as he watched Sarah get into her car.

Cade nodded as he climbed into Brego's saddle.

"Why do you suppose she was so upset?" Matt asked, "Didn't she believe it was an accident?"

Cade shrugged. "I don't think it mattered that it was an accident," he informed him, "I think she's just looking for a reason to hate me."

"To hate you?" Matt looked at him with a confused expression. "Why would she want to hate you?"

"Because I asked her to marry me a long time ago," Cade admitted, nudging his horse towards the tree.

"You asked her to—" Matt seemed to be processing all of this, and he shook his head. "But why would that make her want to hate you? Don't girls usually like that kind of stuff?" he asked, hurrying after Cade.

"We wanted different things, and we couldn't see eye to eye. I left, and she's never forgiven me for it," Cade replied. Then, tossing a rope out of the saddle bag to Matt, he added, "Let's get some of these logs out of the road so Miss Makenna can be on her way, shall we?"

"Ummm...Sure." Matt nodded, hurrying to tie the rope around one of the big logs, but Cade's mind wasn't on his work. It was on the woman sitting there, steaming in her car not ten yards from him. What had happened to them? Years ago, they had been the perfect pair. Everyone had thought so...Until...

"Here you go, Mr. Cade," Matt informed him as he handed the rope up to him.

Cade nodded and took it, tying it to the saddle horn and turning Brego back towards the trail. They had their work cut out for them, but at least, once they got this log moved, it would clear the drive so Sarah could get what she wanted. Brego handled pulling the log like it was nothing, and before long, they had it out of the way. Immediately, Sarah pulled out and sped away, kicking up dust as she did. Cade scowled as he watched her leave. Same old Sarah. Always jumping to conclusions. Never trusting anyone. He was glad she hadn't taken the job here. He wasn't sure he could have handled it.

"Here you go!" Matt declared as he rushed the untied rope back to Cade, leaving the log now in the brush. Cade took it and blew out a breath.

He had a feeling he would never truly understand Sarah Makenna, but in the meantime, he had work to do. And that's what he should be focusing on.

CHAPTER FOUR

"**W**hy'd you have to be so mean to him?!" Josh protested as they pulled out of the ranch and turned onto the road that would lead them into town.

"He deserved it! He put you in harm's way! He was being reckless!"

"He saved me!" Josh argued, "When Brego reared up, I thought I was going to get kicked for sure, but he pulled me out of the way! He saved me, Aunt Sarah, and you yelled at him!"

For the first time since she had seen that horse's legs kicking wildly, Sarah felt her mind clear. She had been so panicked that something might happen to Josh that she had just lashed out. A sense of shame washed over her, and she bit her lip. Perhaps, she had overreacted, but she'd just been so terrified that Josh was going to get hurt and that there was nothing she could do to protect him in that moment.

She shook her head. "You're right. I shouldn't have yelled at him like I did, but he shouldn't have put you in harm's way in the first place."

"But that was my fault," Josh countered, "I ran up there by myself."

She nodded. "I know. You've said that before, but Cade's an adult. He should have taken control of the situation and not just let you do whatever you wanted."

The little boy crossed his arms and muttered, "At least, he let me have some fun."

Her eyes widened, and her mouth fell open. Then, she hung her head and whispered, "I'm trying, Josh."

"You're not my mom," Josh snapped, twisting the figurative knife in her back even more.

Her grip on the steering wheel tightened, and she straightened her back, blinking quickly to keep any tears from forming.

"Well, even so, you're my responsibility, and what I say goes," she declared, trying to make her voice sound firm, "So, no more wandering off without my permission. Got it?"

"Got it," he grumbled, dropping his gaze and kicking at something on the car floor.

"I mean it, Josh," she stressed the words as she looked at him in the rear-view mirror.

"I know," he muttered, and she frowned.

The little city of Hope Town came into view, and she sighed. There was no point in arguing about his attitude. She hoped Josh would listen to her, but she just had to trust him. If she kept pushing him, he was just going to rebel. That much she had learned in her short time as a parent. So, instead of saying anymore, she simply pulled up to the hotel in silence.

After she parked the car, she turned around in her seat, and she stated, "I'm sorry I got so upset before. I was just scared. I thought I was going to lose you."

Josh looked away, staring out the window. Finally, he sighed. "I know. I'm sorry too."

Satisfied that they had settled things, she got out, and Josh did the same.

"Come on, Buddy," she stated, motioning for him to follow as she headed up the steps.

"Are you going to apologize to Cade too?" Josh asked, coming up beside her.

She cringed. So, the matter wasn't settled really.

"I don't know if I'll see him again," she replied, "But if I do, I will."

He looked up at her with a smile, and he nodded his head.

Her body relaxed, and she smiled, glad he was satisfied. Thankfully, she would probably never see Cade again since she wasn't going to take that job at the Wild Hearts Ranch after all.

"So, you wanna' tell me what that was about last night?" Henry asked, leaning against the rails of Fantasma's corral as Cade worked with her.

Cade and Matt had finished removing the rest of the tree from the parking lot just a little while ago, and he had decided to work with Fantasma a bit. But if his boss was in a chit-chatty mood, he had a feeling he wasn't going to get very far.

He eyed Henry out of the corner of his eye as he approached Fantasma with a sugar cube in his hand.

"I don't know," he replied softly, "I guess she still hates horses."

"There was more to it than that." Henry shook his head. "She looked like she would have scratched your eyes out if she could've, but she seemed like such a nice girl before. What happened between you two?"

That was not something Cade was eager to discuss, especially not after what had just happened with Sarah. He shook his head, keeping it vague and simple.

"We dated once, but we couldn't see eye to eye. She gave me an ultimatum, and when she didn't like my answer, we broke up." His jaw tightened, twitching with the memory. No, that was one wild filly he was never going to try to tame again. Never again.

"What was the ultimatum?" Henry asked, raising an eyebrow up.

Cade blew out an exasperated sigh and shook his head. He wasn't going to be able to concentrate until he got Henry to leave him alone. So, he gave up on Fantasma and climbed over the rails, which left him standing next to Henry.

"Well?" Henry pressed.

"I wanted to go into the rodeo, and she didn't want me to," he informed him with a shrug. "I told her I was going, and she dumped me."

"Dumped you?!" Henry scoffed. "By the looks of things, I would have thought you dumped her!"

Cade smirked and shook his head. "Nope, it was all her."

"So, you went into the rodeo, and she went on to run a restaurant. Then, you both ended up back here. Isn't it funny where life'll take you?" Henry chuckled.

Cade nodded. "Yea, I had grand dreams of making it big in the rodeo too, but I guess God had other plans."

"You did pretty good for yourself," Henry pointed out, "And the doctors did tell you that you could head back after you healed from your last accident."

"I know." Cade blew out a breath. Then, motioning around them, he added, "I guess I found something I liked more than the rodeo."

"Well, maybe what Miss Makenna was so upset about last night was that you weren't in the rodeo anymore," Henry stated.

"I don't follow," Cade replied.

"Oh, it's nothing. I was just wondering, if now that you're not in the rodeo anymore, if she's regretting breaking up with you or something. Maybe that's why she turned down my job offer this morning."

Cade scoffed at that, remembering her fiery words before she left. "Yea, I don't think that's it."

"Oh, well..." Henry sighed. "I guess we'll just have to go back to searching for a new cook again."

Cade shrugged. "It's probably for the best."

Henry nodded, looking down as he did. Then, he frowned and pointed at Cade's arm. "What did you do to your arm?"

Cade absently grabbed the arm in question. "Oh, it's nothing. Just a little bruise."

"What happened? It looks pretty nasty," Henry pointed out, trying to get a better look at it, but Cade kept his good hand over it.

"It was just a little accident this morning when we were trying to get the tree cleared for Sarah and Josh," Cade stated with a shrug.

"A bit clumsy around her still?" Henry shot him a teasing look, "Perhaps the old flames of romance aren't as dead as you'd like to believe."

Cade snorted at that and shook his head. "No, they are; trust me."

"Alright, then. So, what did happen?" Henry pressed.

"It was an accident with Brego. He got spooked and accidentally grazed my arm when he started kicking."

"What were you doing standing that close to a frightened horse?! You know better than that!" Henry exclaimed, crossing his arms.

"Yea, but Josh doesn't." Cade replied with a shrug.

"Oh..." Henry held the word as he contemplated all of this. "I see. So, you got kicked saving Josh from standing in front of a spooked horse?"

"Well, yea, I guess you could say so."

Henry smirked at that. "Alright, let me see that arm of yours."

"What?" Cade shook his head. "Why? It's fine."

"Humor me," Henry countered, holding out his hand. "A horse kick is a very powerful thing. You could have cracked a bone."

Cade sighed and held out his arm for Henry to look at. "Don't you think I'd know if it were broken? I've been in this business a long time."

Henry gently touched the bruise, and Cade winced, stifling a hiss that wanted to come out with the pain. Henry let out a low whistle and shook his head.

"Oh, Brego got you good," Henry informed him, "But I don't think it's broken."

Cade nodded. "I told you it's fine. Just a bruise."

70

"Well, you'd better put some ice on that," Henry went on, "That'll help the swelling go down, and I want you to go get that X-rayed just to make extra sure everything's all right."

Cade blew out an exasperated breath. There was no way he had time to wait around the emergency room just to get a bruise X-rayed. He still had a ton of work that he needed to get done today. He was too busy to...

"I mean it now," Henry stated firmly as he pointed a finger at Cade, "I want you to take care of that arm, even if that means I take you to the ER myself."

Cade laughed at that. "No, I'll go. I'll go..." He sighed. "But it just seems like a waste of time."

"Humor an old man and just do it," Henry declared.

"I will," Cade stated, shaking his head. Henry worried too much.

Then, grabbing his gear, he headed for the barn to put it all away, planning on heading out afterwards. Besides, there was a fridge in the break room in there where he should be able to get some ice, but even as he grabbed the ice and put it in a sandwich baggy, he was hit with the thought of all he still had to do yet today. There were several horses that needed saddle broke and a few that were still getting used to listening to a rider's commands. Plus, the back fencing on the forty acres was damaged. That would need repaired at some point. He found some gauze and wrapped the ice to his arm, wincing as he did, but he had to admit the cold felt good on it. That done, he rolled down his shirt sleeve over his makeshift bandage, and he wondered if he could just get by with this. After all, it took forever to get through the ER, and he was fine really. Henry was just overreacting. Cade was alright. Yea, he nodded his head. He was almost as good as new with this ice on it. However, even as he walked out of the barn and towards the next horse's pen, he accidentally bumped his arm on one of the stall doors as he turned to head out of the building. Fire shot through his arm, and he cringed, clutching at it. The pain was sharp and strong, but he willed it away. He swallowed hard and shook his head. Maybe fine was stretching it a bit.

He sighed. He'd better just do as Henry had said. Otherwise, he was going to catch a severe scolding later, and perhaps, it didn't hurt to be safe rather than sorry. So, with that thought in mind, he grabbed his truck keys and headed into town, even if it was going to be a complete waste of time.

Sarah blew out a breath as she finished packing up her suitcase. As fun as this little detour had been, she was ready to get out of town and as far from Cade Jacobs as she could.

Looking over her shoulder, she called, "Are you ready, Josh?"

He came out of his room with his suitcase in hand and his head hung low. He looked up at her with sad, puppy dog eyes and asked, "Why can't we stay at the ranch, Aunt Sarah?"

"This job just isn't the right fit for us," she informed him as she snapped her suitcase closed, "Don't worry. We'll find another place to work."

"But I like this place," Josh whined.

"That's just because this is the only ranch you've seen so far," she informed him, "You'll change your mind when you see our next stop."

"Where's that?" he asked.

She bit her lip. To be honest, she wasn't really sure. She had truly believed that this job was where God had wanted her. So, she hadn't really planned on it falling through. She frowned. Now what? God, show me the way to go, she prayed mentally.

"I'm not really sure," she admitted as she led the way out of the room, "But we'll know it when we see it."

Josh harrumphed as he followed her down the stairs. "Well, if we don't know where we're going, why can't we just stay here?"

She sighed. This argument was going in circles.

"Because we can't," she replied simply as she hurried over to the front desk to pay. The sooner they got on the road, the better. She smiled at the clerk and stated, "I'm ready to settle my bill."

"Of course, let me get that for you," he replied drolly.

"Aunt Sarah, please!" Josh whined, "Can't we stay?"

"No, Josh," she countered, "And that's final."

"Your bill, Ma'am," the man stated, handing it to her.

Her jaw dropped at the sight of the amount. "This can't be right," she protested, shaking her head. She had very limited funds right now, and this bill was going to bleed her dry. "We only stayed here one night!"

"Two nights, Ma'am," he corrected.

"But we didn't use the room last night!" she argued, putting the bill back on his desk.

"That's not my business." He shrugged. "Your luggage was in there, and I wasn't able to rent it out to anyone else. So, the way I see it, you stayed there last night."

"You mean to tell me that I have to pay one hundred and fifty dollars for my luggage to have a room!"

He crossed his arms. "I guess so. People do weirder things."

"But I wasn't planning on staying here two nights. I was going to get a job and check out yesterday, but a tree blocked us in."

"Well, you didn't check out," the man stated simply, "Until now. So, there's the bill."

He slid it over to her. She frowned and angrily dug out her debit card. This was going to eat up her last three hundred dollars. Now, what were she and Josh going to do?

She stiffened her back as she handed him her card. They would just have to hurry to the next job quickly. That was all there was to it.

"Here's your receipt. Thank you for your stay," the man replied in a very fake tone with a smile, "Have a wonderful day."

"Yea, you too," she grumbled. Then, turning to Josh, she stated, "Let's go, Buddy."

Obediently, he followed behind her, surprising Sarah. He had stopped arguing with her too. Maybe he sensed that she was upset and needed a minute, but whatever the reason, she sure appreciated having some quiet time to try and calm herself down.

With a huff, Sarah opened her trunk and threw her and Josh's suitcases back there. Josh trudged over to his seat and buckled up as she headed for the driver's side. She glanced up at the sky and wondered what sort of plan God had in store for her life. It wasn't the first time she had wondered it, but she had been thinking about it much more recently. Her entire life had been upended, and every time she tried to move forward there seemed to be some sort of roadblock in the way. However, there was one roadblock in particular that troubled her the most...Cade. His face popped into her mind uninvited as she turned the key and tried to start the engine, but it didn't turn over. She frowned and pressed in on the brake and tried again. Still nothing. So, she tried revving the gas as she turned the key. Absolutely nothing. In frustration, she smacked the steering wheel and leaned her head back against the headrest.

"Come on!" she snapped as she threw up her arms in defeat. Now, her car wasn't going to work? Why, God? Why are You doing this? she silently prayed.

"What's wrong?" Josh asked from the backseat.

She sighed. "The car won't start."

"Does that mean we can't leave?" Josh asked, a little too excited for this predicament.

"I don't know." She shrugged. "I'll take a look under the hood and see what we're working with."

With that, she popped the hood and got out to take a look, but she had never truly understood engines. Sure, her dad had tried to explain them to her, but unfortunately, she hadn't really paid attention. With him there to handle it, why had she needed to learn? Little did she know he wouldn't always be there. A wave of sadness hit her out of nowhere, and she shook her head, willing the tears to stay away. He had been gone for ten years now, but sometimes the pain felt as fresh as if his accident was only yesterday. She sighed and pulled out the oil dipstick, trying to busy her mind with something even if it was the only thing she knew how to check.

"Do you need some help?"

She jumped at the question. She didn't know why. She and Josh were parked right along the main street. It shouldn't have been so surprising that someone would stop to help, but it wasn't the question or the suddenness of it that had really caused her to jump. It was the voice behind the words. She whipped around to find Cade there staring at her with his arm bound up in gauze. He was the last person she had expected to see. Was he following her or something?!

"What happened to you?!" she exclaimed, her eyes darting to his arm.

"Nothing," Cade stated simply with a shrug before looking away as if he didn't want to talk about that.

"Well, what are you doing here?" she pressed.

"I was just driving by, and I saw you there with the hood up. I thought maybe I could be of some help."

"Hi ya', Cade!" Josh declared from where he stood outside the back of the CRV. "Did you ride your horse here?"

Cade laughed and shook his head. "No, I'm afraid not. Brego doesn't like noisy places like this."

"Josh," she scolded as she turned around, "I told you to wait in the car."

"But Cade's here," Josh whined, "Besides, the car won't start, and it's getting hot." Then, blinking, he asked, "Have you told him yet, Aunt Sarah?"

She opened her mouth to argue, but then she remembered what she had said to Josh earlier. She frowned and turned back around to face Cade.

"No..." she stressed the word, but Josh just crossed his arms. She knew he wasn't going to take no for an answer. So, she cleared her throat. "Umm...Cade," she began, looking away as she did, "I want to apologize for my behavior earlier."

Cade's eyes widened in shock, and he asked, "What?"

"I'm sorry, okay?" she went on, "I overreacted earlier, and I jumped down your throat unfairly. And I'm sorry. I was just worried about Josh."

"Oh, well, you don't need—" he cut in, but she shook her head.

"Yes, I do," she argued, "From what Josh says, you saved him from getting hurt. I should have been thanking you, but instead, I bit your head off. I let our history blind me, and I shouldn't have done that. I was just scared, especially when I saw him there with a horse like that. It was just too much. It sent me over the edge."

He nodded. "I can understand that. I suppose I'm guilty of letting the past blind me too if I'm being honest."

She smiled, her shoulders relaxing slightly.

"Oh, well, good," she replied with a nod, "That's that then."

He smirked at her and crossed his arms. "Thanks for that. I know it couldn't have been easy for you."

She looked away, her cheeks blushing slightly. "It was the right thing to do."

Cade seemed to consider that before motioning with his head towards her car. "What's the matter with it?"

"It won't start!" she complained, kicking at the tire, "I've tried everything."

"Alright," he said as he walked up to take a look under the hood. "I'll see what I can do."

"Thank you, Cade," she admitted as she smiled and took a step back, giving him more room to work. Suddenly, she caught herself, and she realized she was actually glad to see him. Sure, she would have been glad to see anybody in this instance, but it was Cade who had shown up. Years ago, she had relied on him heavily. He had always been there for her, and she had always known she could count on him. Maybe that was part of what had made their breakup so hard.

"Well, here's your problem," he informed her, "You're out of gas."

"What?! That can't be it," she replied, shaking her head, "I just got some this morning."

He shrugged, wiping his good hand that he had used off on his jeans. "Well, there must be a leak in your fuel line somewhere."

"Great," she muttered. That was just what she needed right now. She was broke, and now she had no vehicle. How was she going to get out of here now? She threw her hands down to her sides and shook her head. What was she going to do?

"Aunt Sarah?" Josh asked, tugging on her sleeve.

She looked down at him and blinked.

"Why don't we go back to the ranch?" he asked, "Then, we can stay there for free."

She sucked in a breath as her nephew's logic sunk in. This job, though it meant working with Cade, may be her only hope at giving Josh a good, structured life for the time being. She could just take it on temporarily, just until she had earned enough money to get them to the next place. She considered that before nodding her head.

"Yea, I think you're right," she informed him, "But I just hope Mr. Martin will agree to give me the job back."

"Henry will," Cade replied, as he slammed the hood shut, "He was just telling me this morning how sad he was to see you go."

"I guess, if I take this job, we'll be seeing a lot more of each other," she admitted sheepishly.

He nodded. "I guess so."

"Well, I hope that we can maybe put the past behind us," she offered, "And work together civilly."

He smirked at her. "I'm willing if you are."

She offered him her hand to shake, and in he return, he shook it. But as he did, she got an up close view of his arm. It was swelling and turning red even beyond the gauze he had wrapped around it. Her eyes widened, and he cringed, pulling his hand away. She forced her mind to focus on his injury and not on how good his hand had felt around hers.

"What in the world happened—" she asked, leaning in to see it better, but when he pulled away, she looked him in the face and pressed on, "Did that happen this morning with that horse?"

Josh looked over at her in confusion before following her line of sight, but Cade quickly hid his arm behind his back before Josh could see the large red bruise under the wraps.

Cade took a nervous step back and glanced up at the sky, avoiding her scrutinizing gaze. "It's getting late. I'll call my buddy who works over at the garage. He'll get you where you need to be."

"We've got time, Cade. It's not that late," Sarah objected, pushing closer to him.

She smirked at how he squirmed, looking around for a place to bolt, just like the horses he worked with. He was kind of cute when he was rattled. Cade took another step backwards. "I'm fine," he informed her.

"Then, let me see it," she declared, now standing right in front of him. She held out her hand to him and gave him that same stubborn look she always had when they were kids. It usually worked back then, and she would end up getting what she wanted.

He sighed, looking up at the sky.

"Come on. Quit being a baby and let me see your arm," she demanded, with a hint of teasing in her voice.

"I'm not being a baby," he grumbled, but his posture softened slightly, as a teasing glint filled his eyes. "It's been a long time since you called me that."

She nodded. "Well, it's been a long time since I've had to deal with your stubbornness."

He smirked. "I was always a sucker for when you teased me," he admitted, as he relented and placed his injured arm in her hand.

She peaked under the gauze and inhaled sharply at the swelling and bruising already taking place there.

"Is it broken?" she asked.

"I don't think so, but Henry wanted me to get it X-rayed. So, that's where I was heading when I saw you guys here," he admitted.

"This happened when you pulled Josh out of the way, didn't it?" she asked him softly.

"Brego didn't mean it." Cade shrugged as he took his arm back. "And it was my fault really. I should have been more careful. I know better."

"I'm sorry, Cade," she stated, their eyes locking. She truly meant it. For a moment, it felt like the years disappeared between them, but when he took a step backwards and dropped his gaze, the moment was broken. She shifted nervously, not sure what to make of what had just happened.

"For what?" he asked quietly.

It took her a minute to realize what he meant, but once she had, she stated, "You got hurt protecting Josh, and I—" Her voice trailed off before she shook her head and finished, "I appreciate it."

Not addressing what she had just said, he cleared his throat and pulled his phone out. "I better call my pal."

"Oh, right, right," she replied, nodding her head and stepping farther back.

She couldn't believe how fast things had changed. This morning she was sure she would rather die than work at that ranch with Cade, but here she was agreeing to do just that because she had no other choice. And here Cade was helping her out. She shook her head, looking up at the sky. Was she crazy for doing this? Or was this somehow all a part of God's plan?

CHAPTER FIVE

Holding Sarah's hand... It had felt so delicate in his as a pleasant warmth passed between them. She had smiled, and it had really seemed like she meant what she had said. He'd had to break away though. He'd needed time to clear his mind. Being that close to her had felt too much like old times. She still smelled like warm vanilla sugar, and he wondered if she still used that same strawberry scented lip balm too. He shook his head. He shouldn't be thinking about such things. Not anymore. Not ever.

He hastily found his buddy from the repair shop's number and called him, walking a few feet away, just trying to put some distance between him and her.

While he was on the phone with his friend, he could hear Sarah talking to Henry on her cell across from him. Apparently, she was explaining to him what had happened and asking if there was anyway she could have her job back. Cade already knew the answer Henry would give. Cade might not like to admit it now, but Sarah had always been an excellent cook when they were dating.

"Hello? You still there?" his buddy's voice pulled him back into reality and away from Sarah's conversation.

"Oh, sorry, Miles," he apologized, "I guess my mind wandered off for a second there."

"Is that what happened?" Miles teased him, "When it went silent there for a minute, I thought either I had lost the connection or you had just died."

"Ha, ha, I'm still alive enough to kick your butt," Cade challenged.

"I'd like to see you try," Miles retorted, "So, explain it to me again. What happened to this car exactly?"

"Oh, right," Cade stated, rubbing the back of his neck, "Well, a friend of min—Well, she's not really my friend. She's more like an acquaintance—I mean, we're going to be coworkers now, which is fine, I hope, but still—"

"I get it," Miles interrupted, "There's a girl. Go on."

"Right, well, her car broke down outside of the hotel," Cade explained, "I think she's got a hole in a gas line somewhere."

"Okay, now see that's the information I like to hear," Miles replied, "I can actually use that info, unlike all that other gobbledygook you were spewing about her."

"Alright, but can you fix it?" Cade pressed.

"Sure, but I don't know that we'll have the parts for it," Miles informed him, "It could be several days before we can get it running again."

"Several days?!" Cade exclaimed.

"Don't worry, Cade. We'll get your girlfriend, acquaintance, coworker, lady all set as soon as we can," Miles reassured him, "But we're pretty packed here with vehicles that need fixing."

Cade's cheeks burned as he shook his head. "She's not my girlfriend, not anymore," he muttered.

"Whatever, Man. I'll send someone over there to collect her ride," Miles informed him, "Catch you later."

"Thanks," Cade stated, "See ya' later."

And with that, he hung up and turned to face

Sarah, who had also finished up her conversation with Henry.

"Well?" she asked, her blue eyes wide with hope.

Cade offered her a smile as he put his phone away. "He's sending someone to come pick up your car now."

"Oh, that's great!" she exclaimed. "I just hope it doesn't take too long to get it fixed. I told Mr. Martin we'd be coming back to the ranch today."

"So, you got your job back, huh?" he asked, trying to avoid telling her the bad news.

She nodded. "You were right. He took me back happily. So, when did they say my car would be done?"

"Well, he said it could take several days depending on what parts they need and their workload," Cade informed her with a cringe.

"What?! Several days!" She shook her head. "How am I supposed to get back to the ranch now?"

Cade sighed. He couldn't believe what he was about to say, but before he could stop himself, the words slipped out.

"I can give you guys a ride," he offered.

"You will?!" Josh exclaimed, wide-eyed, "Can we go, Aunt Sarah?"

Sarah hesitated, and Cade couldn't blame her. He knew he was doing the right thing, but he wasn't sure he wanted to be trapped in the cab of his truck with her for the forty-five minute long drive back to the ranch. He knew they had called a truce, but in his experience, hard feelings didn't just disappear with the snap of a finger. He just wasn't sure he wanted to test their new peace agreement so soon, and yet, he couldn't leave them out here stranded either.

"Come on," Cade declared, motioning with his head towards his truck, "Let's get you guys back to the ranch."

"But what about your arm?" she quickly asked.

"Like I said, it's just a bad bruise. I was only in town to get x-rays because Henry wanted me to, and I will...eventually," he replied, flashing her a smile. "But until then, it's going to take a lot more than this to stop me."

"Yea, I remember."

The words popped out of her mouth so quickly they took him by surprise, and she quickly looked away as if they had surprised her too.

"Let me just get our bags," she stated quickly before hurrying to the back of her CRV.

It had been a long time since he and Sarah had been just friends he realized as he watched her walk away. He hoped that maybe this could actually work out, but after the way she had yelled at him earlier, he was unsure if Sarah Makenna would ever be able to truly forget the past.

Josh hurried over to Cade's truck and climbed right in. Then, he peered out and called, "Aren't you coming, Aunt Sarah?"

She nodded as she hurried along with both of their suitcases in hand, but Cade came up alongside her and took the bigger one with his good hand.

"Oh, I've got it. You don't have to—" she started to protest, but he shook his head.

"I'm not an invalid, Sarah, and in case you forgot, us country boys don't make a lady do all the work," he replied, flashing her one of his lopsided grins.

She smiled, and her heart did a little skip like it had years ago when he smiled at her like that. Immediately, she stiffened and reprimanded herself for the reaction. Cade was trouble for her and her life. She had to keep reminding herself of that. She couldn't risk losing all she had built over a few embers that still smoldered a little between the two of them.

"Thanks," she offered quietly as she dipped her head and hurried over to his truck. She felt Cade's steely gaze on her. He was probably wondering what was going through her head, but she had no intention of telling him. So, she kept herself focused on the task at hand, getting Josh's suitcase up to the bed of the truck.

Cade came up alongside her and hefted her larger suitcase into the back of his truck with ease. Then, taking Josh's from her, he did the same with that suitcase. She offered him a thank you and a smile before hurrying over to climb into the passenger side of the truck.

As Cade slid into the driver's side and started the truck, Josh was nearly bouncing up and down in the middle seat between them.

"You've got a nice truck," Josh announced, and Cade offered him a smile as he pulled out onto the road.

"Thanks. I like it," Cade replied.

"Aunt Sarah doesn't have a truck," Josh informed him, and Cade nodded.

"I know."

"But she's the best cook in the world!" Josh's unexpected praise caught Sarah off guard, and she whipped around to face him.

"Oh, you don't have to convince me." Cade nodded as he stopped at a red light, "We used to be friends so I got to eat her cooking all the time. Cakes, cookies, brownies— you name it, and she probably made it for me."

Josh shot him a quizzical look that she recognized immediately. It was that look a nine year old got when they're about to ask a hundred questions about something they don't understand. She smiled to herself as she got comfortable in her seat. *Good luck, Cade.*

"But if you guys used to be friends, why haven't I met you before?" Josh asked.

"Well, your mom and aunt moved far away, and I was busy so—"

"But you guys aren't friends anymore, right?"

"We—um—well, not like we used to be..."

"Why?"

Cade's forehead creased as the questions just kept coming, and Sarah hid her mouth behind her hand to keep from giggling. It felt nice not being the one hounded by a million questions, and watching Cade squirm made it all the more enjoyable.

"We—ah—lost touch," Cade finally said with a

shrug. It was at least part of the truth. Their breakup had been anything but smooth. After her father's fatal accident during a rodeo show, Cade had informed her that he still intended on pursuing his own rodeo career. She had been scared to death of losing him too. So, she had put her foot down and forbidden him from doing it. She had told him if he loved her he wouldn't want to be in the rodeo anymore, and he had said if she loved him, she would let him go. They had argued, and he had stormed off. The next thing she knew, he was on the rodeo circuit performing in shows all across the country, and she was furious. How could he just up and leave her when he knew how she felt on the subject? She frowned. Then, she'd figured out about Josh, and things had gotten more complicated. She never told Cade though. Not only was she angry with him, but she had also wanted him to choose her because he loved her, not just because he felt he had to because of a baby. Plus, the last thing she had wanted was for Josh to have to endure the pain of losing a father to the rodeo like she had. So, she'd stayed silent when perhaps she shouldn't have, but she had made her choice, and now she had to live with it.

"But don't you have a cellphone?" Josh pressed on, pulling her once more back into the here and now.

"Well, yeah..." Cade's tone was uneasy, like he was unsure of where this question was going.

"How do you lose touch with someone when you both have cellphones?" Josh asked.

Cade sighed. "It's complicated," he replied with a shrug, "You'll understand when you're older."

"Why does everyone always say that?" Josh asked as Cade turned onto the road that would lead them back to the ranch eventually, "Whenever a grownup doesn't want to tell me something, they just say I'll understand when I'm older. Why can't I understand now?"

Cade frowned, and Sarah felt sorry for him. Josh was a born debater. He was good at it, but she wasn't about to stop it now. It was just too cute listening to the two of them together.

"Well, did you ever think that they might be telling you the truth?" Cade pointed out, "That maybe you really will understand when you're older?"

Josh seemed to consider this, but he shook his head. "No, I don't think so. Because if that were true, then you would know how to explain it to me so I could understand, but you can't because you don't understand it enough to explain it to me. And you're a grownup. Am I right?"

"I guess you are," Cade admitted, "Sometimes even grownups don't know all the answers."

"Then, how come they always say I'll understand when I'm older?"

"Well, the way I see it, it's cause they've got hope," Cade offered, peaking Sarah's interest. She wondered where he was going with that.

"Hope?" Josh asked.

"Yea, they believe in you. They think you're going to grow up to be even smarter than they are."

"Really? You think so?"

Cade nodded. "Sure, I do. You're a smart kid. You can grow up to be anything you want to be... Even smarter than me."

At that, Josh smiled wide. He was nearly beaming with pride, and Cade smirked. Sarah smiled at that, grateful for this sweet moment in time. She took it all in, not wanting to say anything to spoil it.

But the longer Sarah sat there listening as Josh talked and talked to Cade, the more tense she felt. The kid loved him, but what would happen if Cade learned the truth? Would he take Josh away from her? Her sister and brother-in-law had been killed in a car accident, taking her secret to the grave with them, and now Josh was hers. If Cade learned the truth, it could jeopardize everything. She had planned on never seeing him again. Thankfully, Cade didn't even seem to have a clue about Josh's heritage, and she wanted it to stay that way. But as she watched him and Josh, she felt a pang in her heart. Was she doing the right thing? If she stayed silent, she was guaranteed to keep Josh forever, but she would also be robbing Cade of the chance to get to know his son.

"Aren't you listening, Aunt Sarah?" Josh's voice pulled her back into reality.

"What?" she asked quickly as she tried to hide what she had been thinking about, "What's the matter?"

He giggled and shook his head. "She wasn't even listening, Cade. See? I told you!"

"I guess you did," Cade replied, cracking a smile even though he kept his eyes strictly on the road. She wondered if he was avoiding making eye contact with her, and that made her nervous.

"What was it that I was supposed to have been listening to?" she pressed, hoping her voice didn't show how anxious she really felt.

Josh beamed proudly at her. "Cade said you were a champion barrel rider when you were young. He even said you won medals. Did you really do that, Aunt Sarah? Huh? Huh?"

She nodded, not sure whether to feel relieved or aggravated at the revealed topic. Why did everything to do with Cade have to revolve around horses?

"I did, but that was a long time ago," she replied.

"Why didn't you ever tell me about it?" Josh asked, tracing a circle on his jeans with his finger, "Maybe you could teach me how to do ride around the barrels, and then, someday, I could win medals too!"

Her heart swelled at that. He actually wanted to do something she had done? He wanted to be like her? It was almost enough to relax her no horse riding rule. Then, she was suddenly struck with a thought. What if Cade had known that that was how she was going to feel? What if he had purposefully brought up the topic just to try and manipulate her into letting Josh ride a horse? Why did he care so much about whether or not she let Josh ride horses?! She scowled. As far as Cade was concerned, Josh was nothing more than a coworker's charge. Why was he taking such an interest in his life? Was he drawn to Josh just like the little boy seemed drawn to him? Would he do the math and figure out the truth? Oh, she prayed he wouldn't. That was just something she didn't think she could bare. *Please God. No. Don't let him suspect a thing.*

Suddenly, as if sensing her thoughts, Cade jumped in and said, "I'm sorry, Sarah. I just assumed he knew, and it kind of slipped out." He shook his head.

Her heart softened at that. So, he hadn't meant it to hurt her or to undermine her parenting. She tilted her head slightly as she studied him for a moment. He was different than she remembered. She remembered him being pigheaded and stubborn and selfish, but maybe he was changing for the better. After everything with her surprise pregnancy and her dad's death, she had hit her lowest point, and that's where she had found God again. After that, she had recommitted her life to Him. Of course, they had both grown up in the same small town church, but if she remembered correctly, God was not someone either of them thought of outside of a Sunday church service. Then, when the hard times had come, she had needed God more than ever in her life, and it had changed the way she thought of their relationship. She had learned that He loved her and wanted to be with her all the time not just on Sundays. She wondered if maybe Cade had had a similar experience.

"It's all right," she replied with a dismissive wave

of her hand, "I would have had to show him my medals eventually."

At that, Josh's excitement jumped up another two notches. "You mean you still have them? So, I can see them?"

She nodded. "They're buried in the attic of Grandma's house somewhere. The next time we go to see her, I'll have to dig them out and show them to you."

"Wow! Real medals!" Josh whistled, "I can't believe you won any! You just don't look like you could've won some."

She laughed, trying not to be hurt by his comment. Nine year old's had no filter, That was a fact she had come to realize since taking over raising Josh.

"Hey, I may not look like a cowgirl anymore, but I was one for many years before you were even born," she stated, poking him playfully in the side.

He giggled and wiggled away from her. "I guess that makes you pretty old!"

She faked a scoff. "Well, I never thought I'd hear the day when someone would call me old!" she exclaimed in an over-dramatic tone. She clicked her tongue. "I suppose that clinches it though. Since I'm old, I might as well face it. Maybe I should start looking into some nice nursing homes around here so I won't become a burden to you."

That just brought more laughter from Josh, and he shook his head, placing his hands up to his face. "Don't do that!" he protested, "You're not old anymore!"

"Oh-good!" She breathed a sigh of relief. "That was the worst two minutes of my life!"

Suddenly, she became aware of Cade's steady gaze on the two of them. They were at a stoplight, and he seemed to just be watching them with a smile on his face. Oh, those steely grey eyes of his nearly froze her where she sat, and for a second, she felt like a teenager again. Her heart kicked up a notch. Cade was still as handsome as ever. In fact, his years in the rodeo had helped him fill out. He was no longer the scraggly boy she had known. He was a handsome man.

Suddenly, a horn blew behind them, and she was startled back into reality. What was she thinking?! Quickly, she tore her gaze away from his and pointed towards the light.

"It's green now!" she stated hastily.

Cade's smile slipped some as he turned his focus back on the road.

"So, it is." He nodded. "I guess I got distracted

listening to you two argue. It reminded me of all the good times we used to have back when we were kids." His smile returned as he pulled the truck forward, and he chuckled, shaking his head slightly as he did. "Do you remember that time that we ditched school to go swimming in the creak?"

"Do I?" She couldn't help but laugh at the memory. "And you had to show off by jumping in from the top of the waterfall!"

"Hey, in my defense I was a ten year old boy. At that age, we love to show off."

"At that age?" she challenged, quirking up an eyebrow at him.

"Hey, be nice," he laughed.

"What did you do?" Josh asked, looking between the two of them.

"Well, there was this spot where the creek went over a little waterfall. It was probably only four or five feet tall. I don't remember. Anyway, I thought it would be so cool to walk across the rocks right at the top of the falls, and with the current trying to knock me into the water below, I figured I'd be big stuff if I could make it."

"Weren't you scared?" Josh asked, wide-eyed.

Cade shook his head. "I was too proud to be

scared. I was out to prove how brave I was. Nothing else mattered."

"Wow!" Josh exclaimed, "What happened next?"

"Well, Cade tried to walk across the rocks. He probably made it about three feet or so. Then, he slipped and fell landing at the bottom of the waterfall with a thud," she laughed, "He was soaked and he cut his foot open on an old bottle that was laying in the bottom of the creek."

"Hey, it might be easy for you to laugh about, but I'll have you know that little cut required stitches!" he objected.

She nodded. "Yea, and as I recall those stitches were what got us all caught for ditching in the first place!" She shook her head. "Boy, I was so mad at you! I was grounded for like two weeks!"

"That seems to be our pattern." He shrugged. "We fight; then we make up. Then we fight, and then we make up. Why do we do this to ourselves? Why do we keep fighting?"

She shook her head. "I don't know. I guess we're both just stubborn."

He smiled at that and nodded. "That we are."

"Speaking of which, do you remember that time

that we ended up playing monopoly all night because neither one of us wanted to concede to the other?" she asked.

"Oh-yeah, I still say you were cheating."

"Cheating?!" she scoffed, "How?!"

"I don't know, but there's no way someone rolls three sixes in a row!" he teased.

She laughed, and for the first time, she realized just how much she had missed this. Sure, she had missed Cade as her boyfriend, but she had especially missed him as her best friend. They had grown up doing everything together with their siblings too. Rodeo families tended to stick together. They were often in the same places at the same time, and it was hard to make lasting friendships with anyone outside the circuit. But with Cade, their friendship had been so easy, and she had never had to worry about whether he was a true friend or not. Then, they had started dating. It had seemed so natural, but now, that was her biggest regret. She had ruined the best friendship she had ever had, but she had always dreamed of having that farmhouse with a white picket fence, flower gardens, and kids with Cade. They'd almost had it too before everything fell apart.

"Can we play Monopoly together?" Josh asked

excitedly, "I have the game in with my stuff!"

Sarah smiled and ruffled his hair. "Maybe sometime later. Once we get to the ranch, I won't have time. I'll have to work on getting us all unpacked."

His shoulders slumping forward, Josh blew out a sigh. "Finnnneeeee....We can wait."

"That's my boy," she stated, suppressing the urge to lean over and kiss his head. "You can even help me put everything away. Then, it'll go faster, and we can play Monopoly that much sooner."

"Really?" Josh stuck out his hand towards her. "Is it a deal?"

"It's a deal," she replied, shaking his hand.

Cade turned on his blinker, and she realized that they were back at the ranch all ready. In a way, there was a part of her that was sad to see this ride come to an end. She had actually ended up enjoying herself after all.

CHAPTER SIX

As Cade helped Sarah and Josh unload their suitcases, Henry came up and smiled at him.

"Well, what did the doctor say?"

Cade shifted slightly and offered him a nervous grin. "I haven't gone yet."

"What? But I thought you went there to—"

"I did, but I got sidetracked," Cade explained.

"It's really my fault," Sarah jumped in.

"Mine too!" Josh added.

"When my car broke down, Cade offered me a lift back to the ranch, and I accepted," Sarah informed him.

"Oh, he did, did he?" Henry asked skeptically.

"Yep, and I'm no worse for wear," Cade offered as he unloaded one bag and set it on the ground before reaching for the next one.

"That's yet to be seen," Henry replied, crossing his arms. "A doctor would be better suited to tell you that."

Cade sighed. "I know. I know, and I'm going. I just had to help Sarah and Josh get back to the ranch. You wouldn't want your new cook stranded, now would you?"

"No, but something tells me you're just stalling," Henry declared, "Look. I know you hate hospitals and stuff, but you've got to get that arm checked out."

Cade blew out a breath and waved him off. "I will. Stop worrying."

Henry shot him a stern look that said he wasn't joking, and Sarah wondered if this was still about what had happened to Cade's mom. Ever since his mom had gotten cancer and ended up in the hospital, it had seemed to her that Cade had developed a fear of the hospital and death itself. Maybe it was just her imagination, but that's at least how it had seemed at the time. Plus, he had started spending a lot of time with her family after his mother passed, which made her wonder what his home life was like. Strangely enough, however, even though they had been dating at the time, he had never told her anything about it. She had always just been left to wonder.

Henry looked as if he were going to argue with Cade more about going to get his arm X-rayed, but Cade beat him to it by saying, "Well, I guess I'll be going now if you guys don't need anything else."

"No, we can manage from here," she replied, "Thanks for the lift."

"Don't mention it," Cade stated with a smile and a wink that made her heart flutter unexpectedly, "I enjoyed it."

"Alright, but this time, you had better have gone to the hospital by the time you come back," Henry snapped, and Cade raised up his hands in surrender.

"That's what I'll try to do," Cade informed him before heading to the truck with a wave. "See ya' later."

"Be careful," Henry called after him, and Sarah smiled.

It was good that Cade had found this place. They seemed to really care about him here.

Then, Henry turned his attention to her and stated, "I'm glad you changed your mind."

"Well, I feel like God wants me to work here," she replied honestly. That was the only way she could explain why everything had worked out like it had.

"I've been praying for a nice, young cook," Henry informed her, "And I do believe you're it. Come on. I'll help you get your bags inside. Emmie has been cleaning up the cabin all day."

"Oh, she didn't have to do that," Sarah offered.

"Believe me," Henry began, "She wanted to. Just act surprised. I wasn't supposed to have told you."

She smiled and nodded her head as she followed him inside, ready to start this new chapter in her life. It surprised her really considering just yesterday she had wanted to be as far away from this place as possible, but she supposed that was God's handiwork too. She'd come to realize that He had a way of changing our hearts so we'd go where He had called us to.

A few hours later, Cade pulled in once more to the ranch, this time with his arm tightly wrapped in a compression bandage. It still hurt, but he was glad to know that at least it was not broken. Hopefully, now Henry would get off his back about it.

Just then, he heard the supper bell ding, and he wondered if Sarah had cooked it. In truth, he was kind of hoping she had. It had been a long time since he had eaten her cooking, and he had missed it.

As he stepped into the mess hall, he saw all the ranch hands waiting in line, and Sarah and Emmie were in the kitchen, serving up the food. Just as he was about to get in line, Henry walked up beside him and asked, "So, what did the doctor say this time? Or did you make it there?"

Cade smirked at him and replied, "I got it checked out like I said I would, and it's fine. It wasn't broken. So, I didn't need to go anyway."

"Then, what's the bandage for?" Henry pressed.

"To help it heal faster I guess. It's a compression bandage." Cade shrugged.

"Then, I was right." Henry shot him a smug look. "Since the doctor was able to help you, it was good that you went."

Cade smiled and raised up his hands in surrender. "Fine, I guess you were," he stated, "But it still wasn't broken."

Henry shot him a look, but just then, Josh hurried over to him and stated, "Hi-ya, Cade! Did you break your arm?"

Cade laughed and shook his head. "Nope, I just bruised it really well."

"That's good!"

"So, Sarah is already unpacked and cooking?" Cade asked, turning to Henry, who nodded.

"Yep, Emmie told her she could handle it, but Sarah was insistent."

"I helped Aunt Sarah get unpacked!" Josh stated proudly.

"I bet you were a big help," Cade offered.

"Mommy always said I was," the little boy stated, but as he did, his face fell.

Cade frowned as he felt a pang in his heart. He knew that pain all too well himself.

"Well, she was definitely right," Cade replied, hoping to somehow cheer him up, "She sure would be proud of you."

"You think so?"

Cade nodded.

Josh seemed to consider this before smiling wide. "Yea, I guess she would. I am pretty great."

"That you are!" Henry declared with a laugh.

Josh stared at Cade's bandaged hand and asked, "Is your hand okay now?"

"Well, Brego's kick packed quite a wallop, but it's just bruised."

Josh's eyes widened even more, and Henry nodded.

"That's why we always have to be careful around horses and listen to those that have more experience with them, Josh," he explained, "They're so big they can hurt you instantly, and they don't even mean too. So, you always have to be careful around them."

Josh nodded. "Okay, I understand." Then, frowning, he added, "I'm sorry, Cade, that you got hurt because of me."

Cade smiled at him and ruffled his hair. "It's alright, Buddy. It was an accident,:"

"Now, how would you fellas' like to join me for some supper?" Henry asked.

"I'm game if you are," Cade stated, turning to look at Josh.

Josh smiled wide. "You bet!"

As they waited in line, Cade turned his attention to Sarah as she worked, and he smiled as he watched her. It was good to see her like this again. She was in her element, laughing and joking with Emmie as they worked. It was a side of her he hadn't seen for ten years, and it suited her. Yea, it really suited her.

Sarah happened to glance over at them, and she

waved. Henry and Josh waved alongside Cade, and his heart skipped a bit.

Oh, Lord, he mentally prayed, *What am I doing? I think I'm in trouble.*

After he'd finished his supper, Cade headed out to Fantasma's corral, where the white horse paced back and forth in irritation. He frowned as he watched her and studied her scars. She had been through a lot, and trust did not come easy for her. She had been just skin and bones when they had brought her onto the ranch, and her back and legs were full of scars from the abuse she had suffered. It was a wonder she was still alive, but she was a fighter like him. He respected her for it, and he wasn't about to give up on her either. He was never one to shy away from a challenge, and she certainly was one. He slipped through the corral fencing carefully, and she studied him. She snorted slightly at him, and he smirked at her.

"Hi-ya, Girl," he began in a calm, hushed tone as he approached her slowly. "How are you doing tonight?"

He carefully pulled out a couple of sugar cubes from his pocket and held them out to her.

She perked up her ears and whinnied slightly. He

smiled. "If you want them, you have to come here."

Immediately as if in response to what he had said, her ears went back in irritation. Slowly, however, the temptation was getting to her now, and she was starting to inch her way towards him, cautiously eyeing him as she did.

She was close enough to sniff the sugar cube in his hand, and he held his breath. She was making progress...finally.

"Cade?"

Immediately, Fantasma whinnied and rushed away from him, and Cade sighed, his head hanging in disappointment. He swiped the sweat from his brow as he turned around to head out of the corral. He knew this would just take time, and he had to work at Fantasma's pace. Still, it was frustrating. At least, she hadn't kicked at him this time. He was making progress, even if he couldn't always see it.

"I'm sorry, Cade," Sarah started again, "I didn't realize you were busy."

"That's okay," Cade replied with a shrug, "She's just skittish."

Josh stood on the rails, watching Fantasma in awe beside Sarah.

"Boy, that's a cool horse!" he exclaimed, "He looks fit for a king!"

"She," Cade corrected, nodding towards the horse, "But I agree with you."

"What's wrong with her?" Sarah asked, before quickly biting her lower lip.

He had a feeling she hadn't come all this way just to ask him about a horse, but he decided to play along and not press her on it.

"She's been through a lot," he informed them, "Her previous owners didn't treat her well, and horses are like people. They can feel trauma and fear the same as us. The body's scars may heal, but scars on the heart take a lot longer. That's why I'm working with her, trying to help her heal some."

"Do you like doing this kind of work? I mean, working with horses like that?" she pressed.

He nodded. "I do."

"But isn't it dangerous?" Sarah asked.

He shrugged. "No worse than the rodeo."

She considered that and bit her lip again.

"Could I learn how to ride on that horse?!" Josh asked excitedly.

"No," Sarah stressed the word. Then, shaking her

head, she sighed and went on to explain, "As we were walking to our cabin, he saw you and this horse, and he just had to come over and say hi. Didn't you?"

Josh nodded triumphantly. "I really like that horse."

"And I thought if I told you we were here, we wouldn't startle you," she informed him, "You seemed like you were concentrating so hard, but I think we still managed to mess up your work."

He shrugged. "That's okay. Fantasma and I are getting to know each other. That's all."

"You're getting to know a horse?!" Josh scoffed and laughed at that, like it was ridiculous.

Cade nodded and crossed his arms, leaning up against the corral fence as he did. "Yea, just the same as I get to know people. Horses have their own likes and dislikes. They get scared, happy, mad, and sad just like us. If you ever want to learn how to ride a horse, you'll have to learn that."

Immediately, Josh's face grew gravely serious as he thought that over. "I'll do it. Can you teach me?"

Cade nodded his head. "Sure, I'll teach you how to get to know a horse. It's easy really. You've just got to know what to look for."

Sarah hugged herself and rubbed her arms as if she were cold, but it wasn't chilly outside. Then, motioning with her head, she informed Josh, "Come on, Buddy. We shouldn't keep bothering Cade all evening. He's got work to do."

The kid started to follow her, and Cade wondered what was wrong with Sarah. She seemed different tonight. He frowned. It shouldn't matter to him. She wasn't his problem anymore.

"Oh, wait!" Josh exclaimed, stopping mid-stride and turning to stare at Cade. "I forgot to ask you before! What did you think of Aunt Sarah's cooking?! Isn't it the best?!"

Cade smiled at that, and he noted how cute Sarah looked when she was blushing. Frowning, he quickly looked away and cleared his throat.

"Yep, it was good," he agreed nonchalantly.

"She's even a better cook than—" Josh's face fell, and suddenly, Cade knew who he was talking about.

Cade straightened and backed up a step, feeling suddenly like he needed to move around a bit.

"Umm...Emmie told me about your sister and Micheal," Cade stated, clearing his throat again. "I'm sorry. To both of you. She was a nice girl, and Micheal seemed like a good guy too."

Sarah nodded. "Thank you. It was so sudden."

"Makes you think, don't it?" Cade declared, "How life can change in an instant like that... Makes all the worrying we do seem kind of pointless, doesn't it?"

"Yea, but it shouldn't be an excuse to risk death all the time either," she countered, "They weren't even doing anything reckless, and they were killed. How many others die needlessly doing something stupid?"

Cade's eyes narrowed, and he crossed his arms. "And what exactly would you label stupid? Horseback riding?"

"Well, when done right, it's perfectly fine, but there is a lot of danger involved. Then, you add in speed and reckless stunts—" She shook her head. "So, yes, I would add that one to the list."

Cade scowled. Gone was the carefree girl from his childhood, and in her stead, she left this controlling woman behind again. Why was she always taking digs at his profession? Just because he hadn't chosen to become a lawyer or a doctor or a millionaire on Wall Street....He shook his head. She didn't approve of him anymore than his dad did. Why was it that people couldn't just accept him for who he was and be done with it? Why were they always trying to change him?

"Yea, but you shouldn't live with such a tight-fisted grip on your life that you don't really live it either," he countered.

She frowned, crossing her arms. "Like I do, I suppose?" she challenged.

He quirked up an eyebrow and shrugged his shoulder. "I didn't say that."

"Well, I don't have to be in control of everything!" she argued.

"Oh, right, I forgot. Just mostly everything," he replied.

She frowned for moment. Then, she surprised him by cracking a smile. "Alright, maybe mostly everything," she admitted.

He couldn't believe she had actually admitted that! He had thought she was going to lose her temper for sure. He inwardly shook his head. Man, this woman could keep him guessing.

"Well, it's getting late," Sarah informed him quickly, "We'd better get back."

"Oh, right. Right," he agreed with a nod.

"Bye, Cade!" Josh called as he and Sarah walked away.

Cade waved at him, but once they were gone, he blew out an exasperated breath. He couldn't figure out Sarah for the life of him, but had he ever really been able to? He couldn't remember now.

He took out the sugar cubes once more and inhaled deeply to calm his breathing. He just needed to push Sarah Makenna as far from his brain as possible. He frowned. Why was that becoming so hard to do though?

CHAPTER SEVEN

It had been a week since Sarah and Josh officially moved onto the Wild Hearts Ranch, and Sarah couldn't believe how much she was actually enjoying herself. She loved cooking for all the ranch hands, and Josh was doing so well in this new environment. He was smiling and laughing a lot now, and he even seemed to be listening to her more. Plus, she and Cade had also managed to see as little of each other as possible while still remaining civil to each other. All in all, it seemed everything was working out here just fine. Maybe this place really was where God had wanted her.

"Aunt Sarah, can I help Cade brush down the horses today?" Josh called from the table where he sat eating his cereal.

"Didn't you do that yesterday?" she asked.

He nodded. "But Cade says it really helps him out, and he told me I was real good at it."

"Really," she corrected his grammar.

"Okay, really," he relented. Then, turning eager eyes on her, he asked, "So, can I?"

She sighed. Well, there was one problem with being here on the ranch. No matter how hard she tried to discourage it, Josh just seemed drawn to Cade. She frowned. Josh had never seemed that drawn to her. Maybe she was making too much of it. Maybe it wasn't because deep down he and Cade shared a family bond. Maybe it was just because Cade embodied everything Josh thought a cowboy should be, and Cade really did. He was like a cowboy from days gone by, just like her father had been. It had been one of the reasons she had fallen in love with him. She shook her head to try and change her thought's direction.

"Can I? Pleeeaaassseeee!" Josh was still waiting on her answer, and Sarah offered him an embarrassed smile.

"Alright, fine, but only as long as you don't bother him," she informed him, "He has work to do the same as me."

Immediately, Josh's face broke out into a huge smile, and he rushed towards the door.

But she wagged her finger at him and called, "Uh-uh-uh! Clean up after yourself, and make sure you brush your teeth and comb your hair first. And don't forget to put on your sunscreen."

He nodded, and as he hurried off to do what she'd ask, she couldn't help but wonder why he loved this ranch so much already. Kelsie and Micheal had always lived in the city near Micheal's work, and Josh had never been to the family ranch either. So, where had this love for all things cowboy come from? A pit formed in her gut as she realized that maybe it was genetic. Her father had never wanted to live anywhere else but his ranch. He had loved everything about it, from the horses to the sunshine to the hard work to the fresh air. Everything about it seemed to agree with him just like Cade...just like Josh.

She sighed. Life had a way of changing things up on us though. Before her dad's death, she had never dreamed she would leave the ranch for the big city either, but she had. It had been too hard to stay around that place without him, and the ranch had held too many painful reminders of Cade too. When her mom had decided to sell the old place, it had seemed like God was closing that door for her. But God had brought her back to this life, and she was starting to really enjoy herself. However, she just hoped she wouldn't live to regret working this close to Cade. It was risky, even if they were on civil terms right now. The last thing in the world she wanted to have happen was for Josh to get hurt.

Just then, there was a knock on the door, and she opened it to find Cade standing there with his hands in his pockets. She frowned. Why was he here?

"Cade?" she asked, crossing her arms as she stood in the doorway. "What brings you here so early in the morning?"

"Morning, Sarah," he stated, tipping his hat to her, "I just stopped by to tell you that my friend over at the repair shop called, and he said your car should be good as new tomorrow."

"Tomorrow?" she repeated in shock, "Well, it's certainly took them long enough."

He nodded. "I know, but they had to send out for the parts. They don't keep a lot of stuff like that on hand with it being such a small town and all."

"I can imagine," she replied, "It's fine. At least, it's fixed now."

She watched him, waiting for him to leave, but he stayed put, his eyes searching the ground as if he were trying to work up the nerve to say something else. She studied him closely, wondering what was on his mind. Fear snaked its way up her spine. What if he had questions about Josh?

"What's wrong?" she asked, unable to bear her own suspicions any longer.

"Oh, umm...well..." He cleared his throat. "I think Josh's doing really well with the horses lately. They really take to him. He's a natural, and I know he's really hoping I could someday teach him how to ride. So, I was wondering—"

"No," she snapped, placing her hands on her hips as she glared at him, "We've been over this."

"Well, I don't get why not," Cade pressed, "I mean, you learned how to ride when you were younger than him."

"That was different," she snapped.

"I guess it's your business..." he started.

But before he could say more, she jumped in, "Well, it certainly isn't any of yours."

Her cheeks flushed, and her ears got hot. She crossed her arms and shook her head. Why did Cade always have to push her?

"No, I guess it's not, but that kid wants to ride. It's in his blood whether you want to deny that or not," Cade replied in his simple matter-of-fact way. Why did he always get like that when they were having an argument!? It drove her nuts! Why couldn't he just get upset and start yelling so it wouldn't make her feel like the villain if she did!?

"And if I let him ride, what then?" she argued. "My father was killed riding a horse! How do you know that won't happen to Josh?!"

"I don't, but he wants to ride," Cade countered, "And I'm just warning you that he's gonna' do it, even if he has to sneak around to do it, but that's when it's dangerous."

"And what makes you so sure he'd even try to ride without my permission?" she challenged.

He shrugged. "Because I would have when I was his age."

"What?" She felt her face pale as she weighed his words. Why was he comparing Josh to himself?

"I'm just saying boys his age are starting to figure out their own minds, and they can be difficult to handle. So, I was just thinking that you might want to pick your

126

battles, and let him win a little this time."

"Josh isn't you," she snapped, though the irony of that statement made her wish she'd chosen a different argument. Josh was a lot like his father, whether he knew it or not.

Cade shot her a sideways glance and asked, "Why are you so scared?"

His words caused her to freeze, and her breath caught in her throat. How did he do that? She used to think it was cute how they could almost read each other's thoughts, but now she just found it annoying. She didn't need to explain herself to him, and she certainly didn't want to come right out and say she was afraid of letting Cade and Josh spend too much time together because she was afraid it would reveal her hard kept secret!

"I'm not scared," Sarah lied, crossing her arms and looking away.

"Why did you even take a job at a ranch, knowing how much Josh would want to ride, if you knew he couldn't?!" he argued.

The accusation caused her to clench her fists.

"I can work here without him riding a horse," she argued.

"Yea, the same way a drunk can stay sober in a

bar," Cade scoffed.

"Oh, you think you know all the answers, don't you?!" she snapped.

"Well, in this case, I think I do," he replied matter-of-factly.

She shook her head. "You always think that."

"Have you ever stopped to consider maybe I'm right?"

"Have you ever considered minding your own business?!"

Shaking his head, he laughed and stated, "I don't know why I thought this would be awkward— you and me working together...It's just like old times...You yelling at me about not riding horses...."

"And you not listening to a word I said..." she jumped in.

He smirked at her. "I listened to every word you said. I just don't buy it 'cause you don't make a lick of sense. I thought you'd see that eventually, but..." He shrugged as he turned to leave.

"Well, if I was so wrong, why aren't you in the rodeo circuit anymore?!" she called after him.

She saw his back stiffen as he walked a few more steps, but he stopped and turned around to face her one more time, a fire in his eyes.

"I get it. You and I don't see eye to eye on a lot of things. That's clear," he began, "But it's wrong to keep Josh from riding. It's all he talks about. Let him ride, Sarah. Get Henry or one of the guys to teach him. It'd be good for him...And you."

And with that, he shoved his hands in his pockets and walked away.

She blew out an exasperated breath and shook her head, clenching her fists at her side. Why couldn't anything ever be easy with Cade? Why did he always have to meddle like that?! Why couldn't he just leave well enough alone?! She frowned. She shouldn't have said what she had about the rodeo. She regretted bringing that up, but he had made her so angry. She was Josh's guardian now, and she had to watch over him and do what was best for him. Why did Cade have to push her like that? He knew how she felt about horses. She shook her head. That was the problem. Cade didn't care about such things as feelings....not really. He just wanted to work and do what he wanted, and anything that got in the way of that was just inconvenient. But why did he always have to argue with her? She could say the sky was blue, and he would say it was more of a teal! Why couldn't he just say it was blue too!? Why did he always have to contradict her! And now, Josh was involved, and that was something she did not want at all.

"Aunt Sarah, where's my shirt?" Josh's question pulled her out of her thoughts and back into reality.

"Which one?" she called back.

"The one with the horse on it!" he replied, "I wanted to wear it today to show Cade!"

Shaking her head, she blew out a disgruntled sigh as she headed for his room. She just wished she could shake her head enough to get rid of the memory of Cade Jacobs.

Cade dug his heels deeper into Brego, urging him to move faster. What had started out as a simple survey of the trails to see if they were ready for the trail rides that would be happening later on in the day had suddenly become a race to rid his thoughts of Sarah. But the harder he tried to forget, the more she plagued his brain and the faster he would ride. Why did she have to be so confusticating!? Why did everything have to be an argument with her?! He had just wanted to help, to nudge her in the right direction with Josh. He frowned and shook his head. Okay, it was more than a nudge perhaps, but still, she hadn't had to jump down his throat! He was only trying to help! His grip tightened on the reins. Sarah was good at taking his plans and just upending them. This was supposed to be simple. Just check the trails, but his face burned and his heart pounded in his chest. Irritation coursed through his entire body. He blew out a breath. That woman sure could get under a guy's skin!

Why, God? Why her?! Out of all the cooks in the world, why did you have to bring Sarah Makenna here!?

Brego was nearing a turn, and reluctantly, Cade pulled back on the reins, slowing his horse. It wasn't Brego's fault that Sarah was so difficult. He sighed. How was he going to work with her like this?

He shook his head. Out of anyone, she should know that he knew all too well the dangers of riding horses. He'd seen his share of accidents during his stint as a bareback rider and bucking bronc rider, and he'd seen guys who weren't lucky enough to walk away from an accident, just like Mr. Makenna. Even Cade had almost not made it out of the ring the last time he had competed. He had failed a dismount, and his hand had gotten caught in the horse's rope. He didn't remember much after that, except for lots of pain when he woke up in the hospital, and the doctor told him he was lucky to be alive. Lucky wasn't the word he would have chosen. Still, he had recovered, and he was fully healed now. So, he was well aware of the risks. Yet she still wouldn't listen to him. She was letting fear control her like she always did!

He steered Brego around a downed tree limb. Then, he slid down and pulled the hefty branch off the trail. Before mounting up again, Cade pulled out his canteen and took a long swig before pouring some in his hat and offering Brego a drink.

He knew all the dangers that came with riding horses, yes, but he also knew what a difference horses could make in a person's life. Before he had started riding a lot, he hadn't had much hope in life. He had lost his mom, and his dad had started drowning himself in his drinking. Cade hadn't seen much point in living until he started working with Mr. Makenna on his ranch. There, he had gotten his very own horse, and the two of them trained hard to compete in barrel races and any other competition they could get involved in. He had finally had a purpose, and it had changed him for the better. Why couldn't Sarah see that? She was so busy looking at all the negatives, she couldn't see the positives staring her right in the face.

Blowing out a breath, he mounted Brego once again in one swift motion. He didn't know why it bothered him so much. Whatever Sarah decided to do was her business and hers alone. But still it nagged at him that she had dismissed him like she had. He frowned. Maybe that was it. Years ago, she had valued his opinion. Now, she wouldn't be caught dead following his advice.

He sighed, feeling the urge to gallop off into the sunset again, and he patted Brego's neck fondly.

"What do you say, Buddy? You ready for another ride?" he asked, leaning forward in the saddle, and Brego whinnied excitedly in response. He smiled. "Well, then, let's go."

With that, he kicked his heels in, and his horse raced down the open trail. He relished the feeling of the wind in his face, and it made him miss the rodeo. The rush of a fast gallop gave him almost the same feeling as that adrenaline rush he felt every time he got on a horse, knowing it was going to do its best to buck him off. He smiled as he leaned forward and clicked his heels in again, urging Brego to go even faster. He loved this life...Even if Sarah Makenna did put a damper on things.

CHAPTER EIGHT

That evening, Sarah stood over a large pot of mashed potato soup as she added more ham chunks. She wiped the sweat from her brow and exhaled deeply. She was still stewing over this morning, but she was trying her best not to let it ruin her day. She and Cade had agreed to try and work civilly together. It would be wrong of her to hold onto a grudge, even if he did irritate her. She figured she needed to just treat him like any other fellow employee. If someone else had suggested Josh ride horses, she wouldn't have gotten so upset with them, but Cade Jacobs wasn't just some other employee. He was someone she had known for years. Someone she had loved at one time. Someone who had broken her heart. She sighed. Why was it so hard to get that man off her mind?!

When he wasn't being so pigheaded, Cade could actually be fun to hang out with, like that day she and Josh had road home with him in his truck. It had been nice talking with him and reminiscing about old times. Henry had also told her recently that Cade was going to church again and had been baptized shortly after he had healed from his accident. She wondered if he had recommitted his life to Christ. If so, she shouldn't be quarreling with him so much she supposed. He did really seem to be trying to live his life for God...Just like her. She blew out a breath. Maybe he hadn't been trying to meddle earlier. Maybe he really was just trying to help. Had she over reacted again?

A bubble burst in her soup pot and the fire began to hiss, telling her that it had started to boil over, and she immediately turned off the heat and began stirring it quickly, praying it wouldn't burn. This was her first night cooking without Emmie helping prepare part of the meal. There had been a lot of differences from cooking in a restaurant to cooking here, and Emmie had shown her how to prepare enough food to feed everyone quickly. Sarah was on her own now though, and she just prayed she hadn't messed it up already!

"Hey, Aunt Sarah, how much longer until supper?

I'm hungry!" Josh asked as he walked in and hopped up on the counter across from her.

"It's almost done," she stated. Then, grabbing a spoon, she gathered a bit of the soup and offered it to him. "You want to be my taste tester?"

"Is it mashed potato soup?" he asked, tilting his head.

She nodded. "Mmm...hmmmm."

"Then, you bet I do!" he exclaimed excitedly.

Grateful for the distraction from her thoughts, she laughed as she handed him the spoon, and he hastily put it into his mouth.

"Careful! It's hot!" she warned a bit too late.

He huffed and puffed, trying to cool the hot potato soup in his mouth, and pretty soon, he swallowed it. She cringed slightly. Most mothers would have thought to warn their kids about the food being too hot before they had burned their mouths, but not her. She sighed. Would she ever really be a good mom?

"It's great, Aunt Sarah!" Josh exclaimed, "Can I have some more?"

"What? Didn't you just burn your mouth?" she asked, wondering why he would want to go through that a second time.

He smirked at her and dismissed her with a wave of his hand "Me? It'd take a lot more than that to burn my mouth! I've eaten pizza rolls hotter than that!"

She smiled at his response, but before she could say anything, she happened to notice the crowd of ranch hands and other staff pouring into the mess hall. She needed to hurry. So, she quickly dished up a bowl for Josh and handed it to him with a kiss to the top of his head. Then, she rushed over to get the rest of the soup ready for everyone else's supper.

"Need any help?" a familiar voice asked from behind her.

She spun around to see Cade standing in the doorway, leaning on the door frame and looking between the two of them. Her shoulders relaxed for a moment, but just as quickly, she stiffened again, her back straightening. What was he doing here? Had he come to pick a fight with her now of all times?

She shook her head, but remembering he had offered to help, she gave him a slight smile before saying, "No, I'm almost ready. I'm just having Josh be my taste tester."

"Ah, man! I'm too late to be the taste tester!" Cade exclaimed in an over-dramatic way that made Josh giggle. "That's no fair!" Then, turning to Josh, he asked, "Hey, do you wanna' switch jobs?"

"What's your job?" Josh laughed.

Cade frowned and kicked at nothing on the ground in particular. "For the last hour, I've been stuck behind my desk filling out a bunch of paperwork."

"Bleh!" Josh protested, sticking his tongue out and shaking his head, "I'm not trading jobs for that!"

Cade laughed and nodded. "I can't say I blame you." Then, his cool grey eyes zeroed in on her, and the steely calm focus of them was almost both unnerving and comforting at the same time, like he could somehow read her thoughts and know just how she was feeling. "I'm serious about the help. If you need anything just ask."

"But if I can't make it through a simple meal on my own," she informed him, "Then, I don't deserve to be here."

He smirked at that. "Same old Sarah. Alright, have it your way." He shrugged, his gaze dropping to the floor. "I guess...That was just sort of my way of trying to apologize for earlier."

That stopped her mid-stride, and she turned around to face him. "What?" Surely, she hadn't heard

138

him right. Cade Jacobs couldn't be apologizing to her?! He never apologized!

"Apologize for what?" Josh asked with his mouth full.

"Your aunt and I had a disagreement earlier, and while I was doing all that paperwork, I realized I didn't handle it very well," he admitted. Then, turning his gaze back on Sarah, he added, "I shouldn't have pushed you so hard, and I'm sorry."

She was speechless. She knew she had to say something, but what?! This was the last thing she had expected from him! Finally, she shook her head to force her brain to function again, and she stated, "I'm sorry too...For what I said...About the rodeo...That was uncalled for." It was hard to say, but she felt like a weight lifted off her shoulders once she had.

He smiled at her and winked. "No worries, and remember. I'll be just out there if you need any help."

"Thank you, Cade," she replied, her shoulders relaxing as she returned his smile, "I appreciate it."

"Well, you better get a move on," he informed her, "How else am I going to be able to get seconds?"

"Seconds? You haven't even had firsts yet. How do you know you'll want seconds?" she asked, shaking her head in mock annoyance.

"I don't have to have had any," he replied as he turned to leave, "I've tasted your cooking before, remember? I know I'll enjoy it."

And with that, he waved his hand and disappeared down the hall. With him gone, she felt like the room had grown slightly colder, or maybe there was just a draft. She shook her head. She was just focusing on anything but what she needed to be. She couldn't obsess over all of this. Sure, Cade had apologized, something she had never thought she would ever see happen, but that didn't change things between them. It couldn't, not with Josh's happiness at stake. She shook her head. She needed to focus on getting this supper going and nothing more. She sighed as she grabbed her pot holders and prepared to move the soup. Had Cade really changed as she had? Could things truly be different between them if the past was haunting them?

She finished pouring out the soup into the serving pans, and she took the biscuits out of the oven and sat them on a serving tray. Then, she checked the other ovens and realized the dessert she had prepared was almost finished. She hoped everyone liked Texas sheet cake. That done, she took one last step back to admire everything and make sure it was right. She breathed a sigh of relief when everything appeared to be in order. She had done it. Reaching for the dinner bell, she was about to ring it when the sight of Josh sitting there staring at her stopped her in her tracks. She offered the cowbell to him with a smile.

"Do you want to ring the bell and tell everyone it's time for supper?" she asked.

"Sure, Aunt Sarah!" he exclaimed, rushing over, and he rang that bell as hard as he could.

As soon as that cowbell tore through the air, the line began to form, and there was a steady hum of people talking and moving along in line. Sarah prayed a quick prayer that everything would taste all right, and she watched as some of the first people took a bite of their soup. From the smiles on their faces and the way they started to dig in afterwards, she finally released the breath she hadn't realized she had been holding in and smiled. They liked it. They really liked her cooking.

"It appears everything is going off without a hitch."

She was startled by the voice behind her, and she whipped around. Just as quickly though, she relaxed at the sound of his laugh.

Henry shook his head and raised up his hands. "I didn't mean to startle you. Sorry about that. I just came in to see how everything was going."

She nodded, daring to glance once more out into the cafeteria. "It's going well," she admitted.

"That's great! I'm glad to hear it!" Henry replied, "Oh, and I also stopped by to let you know that I have a friend who works at the local school, and they said that Josh is welcome to attend there at any time. I mean, if you two decide to stick around that is."

Josh stuck his tongue out. "Eww...School."

Sarah realized with horror that she had forgotten all about school for Josh! With all the chaos she had been having to deal with lately, she had completely forgotten about that! But how could a mother forget something so important?!

"Thank you for doing that for me," she replied, "I should have been looking into that before now, but I've been so busy."

"Don't worry about it," Henry replied with a wave of his hand, "You two weren't even sure if you were going to stay. This is just my way of trying to entice you guys to stick around. You're doing a fine job, Sarah, with both the cooking and Josh. My wife says I'm incorrigible, but I just can't help it. When I like people, I want to help them, and you two, I like a lot. I wish you'd change your mind about leaving soon and stick around."

She smiled and nodded her head. "Well, I'm beginning to think we're going to do just that," she admitted, "It seems like God wants us here. So, we'll try it."

"Oh, that's wonderful to hear!" he exclaimed, clapping his hands together. Then, handing her a piece of paper he'd had in his back pocket, he stated, "This is all the contact information for the school, and my friend's number. She should be able to get Josh enrolled with no problems."

Sarah smiled as she took the paper and placed it in her own pocket. "Thank you, Mr. Martin. I really appreciate it."

"Oh, don't mention it, and call me Henry," he replied, "Everyone else does!" Then clapping his hands together, he added, "Now, I'd better hurry up and get in line before all that good grub is gone."

"Don't worry. I've still got more soup simmering on the stoves. I made a lot, probably more than I needed too, but I wanted to be sure I had enough," she answered.

He nodded. "Trust me. There's never too much food on a ranch. There's always someone hungry enough to eat it." Then waving, he headed out to the mess hall to grab a plate.

She smiled to herself and breathed a prayer of gratitude to God. Things were beginning to fall into place, even things she had forgotten about. Maybe this really was where God wanted them after all.

"Do I have to go to school, Aunt Sarah?" Josh asked.

She nodded. "I'm afraid you do if we're going to stick around here," she informed him.

He scowled at that and sat his bowl down. "But I don't want to go. I want to work on the ranch with you and Cade."

Sarah sighed. Well, she supposed not everything could be perfect.

"Come on, Josh. It won't be that bad," she offered.

He crossed his arms and looked away from her, and she frowned.

Then, remembering something that might make this all better, she hurried over to the oven and pulled out one of the Texas sheet cakes. Cutting out a big piece, she topped it with some homemade chocolate frosting, and she handed it to him.

"Will some cake make it better?" she asked, her voice full of hope.

He eyed the cake and glanced at her before smiling and nodding his head.

"It's a start," he reasoned.

She smiled, grateful he seemed to have perked up, but she had a feeling this wasn't the last she was going to hear of this school argument.

Sarah's supper had gone off without a hitch as Cade had known it would, and now, everyone had left the cafeteria to go their own way. Most of them were hanging out around the large porch that ran in front of the cafeteria, playing instruments and gossiping, but not Cade...No, there was still more work to be done, and he couldn't stand idle chitchat either. He didn't mind talking, but when there was work to do, he couldn't just ignore it. He passed by Stardew's stall and checked in on her. She was going to foal soon, but the time hadn't come yet. He would have to keep a close eye on her over the next couple of days.

Once again, he heard the sounds of the guitar

strums floating through the air, and he shook his head. He yawned, unable to stop himself. He really should call it a night soon, but he still wanted to check in on Fantasma and some of the others before he did.

"What are you doing?" a familiar voice asked.

He turned around to find Josh, popping his head up over one of the empty stall's walls.

"I could ask you the same thing," Cade replied, stifling a laugh as he crossed his arms. "It's getting late. Shouldn't you be in bed?"

"It's only nine o'clock," the little boy protested as he walked out of the stall to join him in the middle of the barn.

"On a ranch, that is late." Cade winked at him. "We get up before the sun does around here."

"Why would you want to do that?" Josh's brow furrowed, and this time, Cade couldn't stop the laugh from coming out.

He shrugged and stated, "I don't really know."

"Then, why do you do it?" Josh pressed.

Cade thought on that and shook his head. "Well, the animals like to be fed that early, and you can get a lot of chores finished before breakfast that way."

Josh stuck his tongue out. "Chores..." He

shuddered.

"Oh, come on," Cade insisted, "Chores aren't that bad."

"Chores are as bad as school!" Josh argued with a frown. He looked away, crossing his little arms across his chest, and Cade realized something must be bothering him. After all, he had seemed to love to help with chores before now. What had changed? Then, he realized Josh had mentioned school, and earlier today, he remembered Henry had talked about how he was hoping his friend could get Josh enrolled in the local school. Maybe that had the kid upset for some reason.

Deciding to pursue his hunch, Cade asked, "So, school, huh?"

"Aunt Sarah says I have to go to school here!" Josh snapped.

Cade blinked. "And you don't want to?"

Josh shook his head adamantly. "All schools are the same! They just babysit you until your parents get back from work!" His hands balled into fists. "And the other kids...they always make fun of you!"

Cade frowned. He hated the thought of Josh getting bullied. Like it or not, he was attached to the little guy.

"So, you were bullied at your other school?" Cade asked.

"Mom said they were just jealous," Josh informed him with a scoff, "But if they were jealous, I don't know of what. I suck at everything."

"Hey, come on," Cade protested, "I'm sure that's not true! You're great at a lot of stuff."

"Oh, yeah? Like what?" Josh pressed, "All the kids used to say I was a loser because I never made any of the sports teams. I don't get great grades, and I stink at art! What am I great at, Cade? What?"

"Well, you sure can argue, I'll give you that," Cade replied, and that at least got a slight smile out of Josh before the scowl returned.

"I'm serious," the little boy reminded him.

"So am I. And you're great at lot of things. Just like brushing down the horses. Not everyone can do that, but the horses love you. You're a natural," Cade replied.

Josh's eyes widened. "I am?!"

Cade nodded, and he motioned for Josh to sit on a nearby bench with him.

After they were both sitting down, Cade stated, "Look, Kid. I know it can be tough going to school. I was bullied too."

"You were?!" Josh exclaimed.

Cade nodded. "I was."

"Then, why would you want me to go back to school?!" Josh argued, "You know how horrible it is!"

"But I also know how important it is," Cade replied, motioning around them as he continued, "Even on a ranch like this you have to use what you learn in school. Did you know that?"

Josh shook his head, and Cade went on.

"Say, I want to trade a horse with someone, I have to use math to figure out how much money to charge them and how much money I should have after they pay me, right?"

"Well, I guess so."

"And it wouldn't look very nice on all the stall doors if I misspelled the horses' names, now would it?"

Josh giggled and shook his head. "No..."

"See? Plus, most importantly, you'll keep learning how to read so you can read God's letter to you," Cade finished.

"God wrote me a letter?" Josh asked, his eyes going as wide as saucers.

Cade nodded. "The Bible is God's letter to each of us, and school teaches you how to read so you can enjoy it."

"But I already know how to read," Josh argued, "What's the point now?"

Cade blew out a breath. It was not easy arguing with this kid for sure. "Well, um...What about history? There's all sorts of cool things you learn in history in school."

"What kinds of things?"

"Well, like you could learn about the Wild West and like how our nation was started..." Cade's mind raced for other examples from when he was a kid in school. "Plus, there are different wars and stuff like that too, and don't forget about science. You can learn how things work too."

Josh sighed and hung his head. "But I hated my old school."

"This is a new school though," Cade volunteered, "Maybe things'll be different here. In fact, I know they will be," Cade added, straightening up as he spoke.

"How can you be so sure?" Josh asked skeptically.

"Because if anyone bullies you, they'll have to answer to me. How's that?"

Josh's face broke out in a wide grin. "You mean

it, Cade?"

He nodded. "I sure do. I can't have my little buddy getting bullied, now can I?"

Josh relaxed slightly in his seat as he thought this all over, and finally, he nodded. "Alright, Cade. I'll go to school."

"That's great!" Cade smirked at him. "I know you can do it!"

Cade's heart swelled inside his chest, and he couldn't help feeling excited. His advice had actually helped Josh. He had helped steer a little kid down the right road. What a rush! He wondered if this was how parents felt all the time. He shook his head. Why was he thinking of parents? Sarah was just his friend now, not his fiance, and Josh was her nephew and his friend. They weren't a family, and he had no real place in Josh's life. He smiled once more though. It still felt really good to help either way.

CHAPTER NINE

Sarah had to fight the tears that threatened to spill as she listened to Josh and Cade talk. They were having a father-son moment, and they didn't even know it. Cade had somehow managed to convince Josh to try going to his new school when all her words had failed. After supper, she had tried to talk with Josh more about it, but he had gotten upset. He'd gone to his room and shut the door, and when she'd gone in to talk with him, she'd found his room empty. She'd been horrified and had rushed out to find him, but as she did, she had felt like the Holy Spirit had urged her to check the horse barn. Just as she had approached the building, she'd heard Cade and Josh talking, and the more she listened, the more she realized she couldn't break this up. She smiled as a tear ran down her cheek, and she leaned against the barn door just listen to them. Cade had grown up. He was a fine man now. He had handled the school argument better than she could ever have imagined, and now, she didn't expect to have any more arguments from Josh about school. She couldn't believe Cade would do that for her. She had always thought that after their breakup he would certainly hate her forever, but maybe she had been wrong. He had helped her with Josh without expecting anything in return. She swiped at her eyes and shook her head. What was wrong with her? Why did she feel so much like crying? Why did she suddenly feel a huge weight of guilt fall onto her shoulders? Why should she tell Cade the truth? It would ruin the nice relationship they had just started to cultivate again. How could she jeopardize that for something that had happened years ago? She frowned. This secret had the power to change everything. If Josh found out his father was Cade and not the man he believed to be his dad, he would start asking questions about who his mom was, and his whole little world would be shattered. She just couldn't let that happen to him. He had been through too much already for her to let any unnecessary hurt come to him. She shook her head, forcing herself to focus on the task at hand. Cade was a good man, and he had matured from the boy she had known. He was going to be a great dad someday, but she shook her head. She couldn't ever tell him about Josh. She would keep this secret no matter how painful it was in order to protect them all.

She realized Cade and Josh were starting to wrap up their conversation, and she forced herself to focus on the here and now. She needed to get Josh back home and get him in bed for the night. Tomorrow, they would have to go to the school and fill out all the necessary paperwork for him to enroll there, and she wanted him in the best mood possible for that.

Still, she hesitated. She hated to break up this sweet moment, even if it was already coming to a close, but she knew she had to. Still, she didn't want them to know she had been listening either. So, she took several steps away from the barn and started calling for Josh as if she were still looking for him. Then, she headed straight for the barn, hoping they would not have a clue that she had been eavesdropping on them all this time. When she crossed into the barn, she placed her hands on her hips and scowled at Josh.

"What are you doing in here, Mister? I went to your room, and you weren't there," she stated, trying to keep her voice sounding firm, "What have we talked about sneaking out, hmmm?"

Josh nodded his head as he stood up. "Sorry, Aunt Sarah, I was just coming back to the house. I'm not upset anymore. Cade and I talked, and I decided I'll go to school after all."

"Well, good for you," she informed him with a smile, "I'm glad to hear that."

She was so relieved she wasn't going to have to fight with him on this. Any time she could avoid an argument with Josh, that was a win in her book, even if it wasn't her that had won the battle but Cade. "Hurry on up to the house now, and I'll be right behind you to tuck you in, okay?"

"Alright, Aunt Sarah," he replied as he headed out the door and out into the evening air.

She watched him leave for a minute, but then, Cade pulled her focus back to him by saying, "He's a good kid."

She nodded. "He's been through a lot, and he likes to act out because of it. But he's still a great kid."

Cade smiled and turned to leave, but she quickly stopped him.

"Wait!" she exclaimed, "I wanted to thank you."

The words were harder to spit out than she had planned for some reason. She suddenly felt like she had cotton mouth.

"For what?" he asked, tilting his head, and her heartbeat kicked up a notch. For what indeed!? She wasn't supposed to know about his heart to heart with Josh. What was she going to do now? She needed to think fast..Then, she remembered what Josh had said, and she saw her way out of this.

"Well," she explained, "Based on what Josh said, you obviously convinced him to go to school after all. When I first brought up him going to school this evening, he hadn't taken it very well."

Cade gave a simple one shoulder shrug. "Oh, that? It was nothing."

"It's something to me, and I really do appreciate it," she informed him, meaning every word. "I also thought it over, and I've decided to let Josh take horseback riding lessons as a reward for his going to school."

Cade's eyes widened, and his mouth dropped open, obviously stunned by her change of heart. In truth, she was too. But as she had listened to them talk tonight, she'd realized just how much the two of them were alike, and she had suddenly realized Cade was right. By keeping Josh from riding, she was going to lose him. She had to let him do this, and she could use it to help improve his grades too. What better way was there to help him focus at school than to tie that to horseback riding lessons?

Cade shook his head, and he flashed her one of his lopsided grins, winking at her. "That's great! He'll love it. What made you change your mind?"

She hesitated and shifted on her feet. How could she explain it to him? What could she say?

"I thought maybe it would entice him to go to school," she admitted part of the truth.

"Well, if you still don't want him to ride, I don't think you'll have to promise that," Cade offered, "He seems willing to go as it is."

She nodded. "I know, but you made some good points earlier. I want him to be able to learn."

His smile widened, and he nodded his head. "Good for you, Sarah. I'm proud of you. I know it freaks you out, but it's good for you to let go a little."

With that, he once more started to walk away, and she felt the sudden urge to stop him, to talk to him just a little bit more, to be near him like she used to be.

Perhaps, it was the guilt eating away at her. Or maybe it was something else. She wasn't sure. Listening to Cade and Josh as they'd talked together, she had suddenly been struck with the thought that they could have been a family had things ended up differently. Didn't Cade deserve to know that he actually had a son? But could she really tell him the truth?

"Cade!" she called after him, and he stopped to look once more her way.

"Yea?"

Her face flushed, and her courage evaporated when she looked into his eyes. She shook her head, smiling softly at him but quickly looking away from his gaze.

"I just wanted to say thanks again," she replied with a wave, "Good night."

"Good night, Sarah," he returned the sentiment, "I'll see you in the morning. I'm sure you'll have a fine breakfast for all of us."

She laughed and nodded. "Yea, I suppose I will." Then, realizing Josh had probably made it to the house by now, she sighed, "Well, I really should be going."

"See you around, Sarah." He waved at her before turning on his heel and heading farther into the barn.

"Yea, see you around," she offered before hurrying back outside and towards her and Josh's cabin.

Her heart ached inside of her chest, and she shook her head. Why? Why now? For all these years, she had been content keeping Cade in the dark. There were times she could have told him before Josh was born or right after, but she hadn't. She had been angry. She'd wanted nothing to do with Cade, and now thinking on it, she thought maybe she had wanted to punish him too. He had hurt her so badly. She hadn't really been thinking of how much she could be hurting him...until now. Now, she and Cade were starting to become friends again. She was starting to care about him again...in a totally, purely friendly way. She reminded herself quickly, clenching her fists at her side and nibbling on her bottom lip. It could never be anything more. Not now. Not after everything. If he every learned the truth, he wouldn't want anything to do with her. Of that, she was quite certain.

She opened the door to the cabin and found Josh standing in the living room, brushing his teeth as he watched cartoons on the TV. He really wasn't brushing at this point though. More like he was just standing there with a toothbrush in his mouth totally distracted by the show. She had to smile. Oh, how she loved her boy! She just wished somehow he could understand just how much, but she couldn't ruin the memory of his parents by telling him the truth. So, she supposed she would forever be the aunt he'd gotten stuck with. She sighed as she shut the door. That would forever be her cross to bear.

He turned around to face her and smiled. "Ohhh...Andt Saarraah," he stated with his mouth full of toothpaste, "I waas dust brussing my teeth."

"I can see that," she stated with a smile, "You'd better go spit out that toothpaste before you choke though."

He shook his head. "I won't toke."

"You can spit in the kitchen sink as long as you rinse it out that way you don't miss any of your show. How about that?" she asked, and he considered her offer.

Then, he nodded and hurried over to the sink and did as he was told.

She suddenly felt very weary as she glanced up at the clock. It was only nine-thirty, but she felt like it was much later. She had had a full day, and all the stress and excitement was wearing on her. She smiled to herself. She hadn't gone to bed this early since she'd left her parents ranch all those years ago. She supposed it just went hand and hand with ranch life.

The credits started playing on Josh's show, and she clapped her hands. "Alright, time for bed."

He sighed, his little shoulders drooping. His blue cowboy pajama pants didn't match the red super hero shirt he had picked out, but he still made an adorable sight.

"Before you head to bed though, I've got something else to tell you," she began.

"What's that?" he asked, sounding slightly nervous.

She smiled. "Well, I know going to school isn't something you really want to do, but how would you like to take horse riding lessons after school every afternoon as a sort of reward?"

"You mean it?!" he exclaimed.

She nodded. "I do, as long as you keep going to school without any arguments and you do your homework and get good grades."

"I'll do it! I'll do it all, Aunt Sarah!" he nearly shouted, rushing over and hugging her tightly, "Thank you! Thank you so much!"

She laughed and hugged him back, grateful for this moment with her boy. "It's alright. I love you, Josh."

"I love you too!" Josh stated happily.

"Now, it's time you get to bed, young man," she informed him, "We've got a big day tomorrow."

"Alright, I will," he replied, hurrying towards his room, but he stopped at the door and turned to face her, "What horse will I get to ride?"

She laughed and shook her head. "I don't know."

He shrugged. "Oh, well, I don't care as long as I can ride one," he informed her.

She nodded and watched as he disappeared into his room. Perhaps, she had made a mistake telling him about this tonight. She had a feeling he wasn't going to get much sleep now. He was nearly bouncing up and down with excitement.

She smiled, but then, fear began to snake its way up around her heart. Panic began to threaten her, and she had to remind herself to inhale deeply. Keep breathing. That was all she had to do. She was fine, she reminded herself. She had just had a busy day. She was exhausted. Her brain was weary. She couldn't let herself have a panic attack. Not now.

She silently prayed that Josh would be safe when he was riding. She knew she was doing the right thing, but why was it so hard? She had made Josh so happy, but why did it have to scare her so much?

She shook her head, willing herself to focus on anything but the fear. She needed to get ready for bed. That's what she needed to focus on right now. Yet still her mind played tricks on her as she tried to sleep.

Images of her and Cade and Josh living like a normal family danced through her dreams all night long.

CHAPTER TEN

The next morning, Cade paced back and forth outside of Sarah's cabin, wondering what he was doing here. All night long, he had been thinking about Sarah's sudden change of heart. She was going to let Josh ride horses! Even though she was scared, she was going to do what was best for him, putting his needs before her fears. That was quite the change from the woman he had used to know.

When she was terrified of losing Cade after her dad's death, she had tried to control everything about his life with a choke hold grip, including him, and like a wild mustang, Cade had run as fast as his legs could carry him. But now...Now, she was different...At least, she was trying to be. He was sure this wasn't easy for her, but she was still doing it. He smiled to himself.

Maybe things between them could be different too.

He inhaled deeply and set his jaw in a determined line as he clenched his fists. He had to do this. He would kick himself for the rest of the day if he didn't. He blew out a deep breath and turned to face the door. This was it. Would she think he was stupid? Or annoying? Or forward? His frown deepened. Would she laugh in his face? Or would she appreciate the gesture? He shook his head. He couldn't stand around here all day thinking of the what if's! He needed to act! He just prayed for the courage to do so.

He put one foot slowly in front of the other, and before he knew it, he was in front of her cabin's door, his hand poised to knock. He needed to do this. Seeing the change in her last night had given him hope that maybe —just maybe—they could be really good friends again. After all, he had missed having her in his life, even if she could be a domineering pain in the butt from time to time, and he was really enjoying getting to know Josh too. Was it wrong of him to want to be their friend? He tilted his head as that thought needled at him. That's all he wanted, right? What did he really hope to get out of this? Friendship? Or something more? He shook his head not wanting to dwell on that. That was a closed chapter in his life, and that breakup was not something he wanted to repeat. He just wanted to be friendly...That was all... He hoped.

"Here goes," he whispered.

Suddenly, before he could actually knock, the door flew open, and Sarah and Josh were suddenly standing right there, with Sarah's face ending up right in front of his fist.

"Cade?!" she exclaimed, nearly frozen at the sight of him.

He cleared his throat and shook his head as he hastily dropped his arm back down to his side. "Good morning," he began nervously.

"Good morning!" Josh declared happily with a wave.

"Good morning," Sarah added, glancing around as she took a step back and looking slightly confused by his presence here.

He needed to say something fast to explain himself, or he was going to completely blow this chance.

"That was some breakfast this morning, Sarah," he offered, tipping his hat to her. "You out did yourself."

He frowned, inwardly chastising himself. That wasn't what he was supposed to say! Why couldn't he bring himself to spit out what he had come all the way over here to say? But that fear that she might say no stopped the words in his throat!

"Alright, Cade, spit it out," she stated, crossing her arms, but there was a teasing glint in her eye as she playfully punched him in the shoulder, "You didn't come all this way just to wish me a good morning and tell me I'm a good cook. What are you really doing here?"

He smiled at the unexpected gesture, and he suddenly forgot what it was he had wanted to say. What was it again? He shook his head to clear his thoughts and force himself to focus. Suddenly, he remembered, and he inhaled a deep breath. It was now or never. Win or lose, he had to say it. He had to try.

"I—I was just wondering if—maybe—you and Josh needed a ride into town," Cade offered, rubbing the back of his neck as he did. "I mean, your car is ready to be picked up, but you don't have a way to get there yet, and I thought to myself, why not I be a good neighbor and offer to help?"

She smiled and nodded. "Thanks, Cade, but Emmie already said I could borrow her car, and I don't want to put you out a second time. You've already done so much," she answered, and his chest tightened slightly.

He'd known she would probably say no, but he had still hoped maybe she wouldn't this time. He'd hoped maybe just maybe she would have been happy to spend some time with him.

He frowned. He needed a new plan of attack; otherwise, she was just going to leave.

"Well, if I drive you in, then you can pick up your car without having to leave Emmie's behind when you drive home," he informed her, grateful for the argument that had just come to him.

She stopped and considered this. "I hadn't thought of that."

He nodded. "Besides, you're really not putting me out at all. I have to go into town for some supplies anyway, and I'd love the company."

"I have to go to the school with Josh to get him all registered," she replied, twisting a loose strand around her finger absently. Her resolve was wavering.

"That's fine. I don't mind waiting around for a while. How long could it take?" he declared with a lopsided grin. He didn't know why it meant so much to him, but he prayed that she would say yes. He wanted a chance to get to know her again, to see how much she had changed and how much she had stayed the same.

She tapped a finger to her chin as she thought it all over. It was the longest thirty seconds of his life! Finally, she nodded her head.

"Alright, you've convinced me," she replied, "We'll ride in with you."

"Yea!" Josh exclaimed, rushing up to Cade and giving him a high-five, "This is going to be fun!"

Cade smiled at that and ruffled Josh's hair, but when he turned to face Sarah, he was surprised to find her nibbling on her lip and looking at nothing in particular on the ground. She seemed suddenly lost in thought, and he wondered what was wrong. But before he could ask, she seemed to have snapped out of it, and she smiled at him as she marched towards his truck. "Let's go, shall we? I don't want to be late."

"I don't care if I'm late," Josh protested.

"But I do. Now, come on, you silly goose," she called with a laugh.

Cade smiled and leaned down so only Josh could hear.

"We'd better do as she says," he informed the kid, "It's easier to just do it than to sit around and get the lecture that's comes if you don't."

She whipped around and shot him an "I heard

169

you" look, and he laughed sheepishly.

"Well, it's true." He shrugged with a laugh.

She playfully shoved him and shook her head. "You're impossible!" she declared, but she was still laughing. He smiled to himself and tapped Josh on the arm.

"Come on. Let's get going," he informed him.

Josh smiled wide. "Alright, I'll race ya'!" And with that, he took off at a full sprint for Cade's truck.

Cade ran after him, but his focus wasn't on winning. His eyes watched Sarah as she made her way towards his truck, and he wondered why she seemed so different today.

Josh slammed his hands into the bumper of the truck and declared triumphantly, "Ha! I win!"

Cade laughed and nodded his head. "Okay, I admit it. You won." Then, matching his stride with Sarah's, he just walked along beside her.

She glanced over at him and smirked. "Thanks for offering to drive us into town."

"Thanks for accepting," he replied, bumping into her slightly, "I wasn't sure if you would."

"I almost didn't," she admitted, bumping him back, "But then I figured we're just hanging out as friends. So, what's wrong with that?"

"Right." He nodded, but for some reason, that comment let some of the wind out of his sails. He shook his head. He didn't want to analyze why though.

"Hey, Cade, after we get done at the school, can I help you groom some of the horses again?" Josh asked, turning to stare at him with big eyes.

"Sure, as long as it's okay with your Aunt Sarah," Cade declared.

"Is it, Aunt Sarah? PLLLLEEEEAAASSSEEEE!" Josh begged.

She laughed and nodded her head. "As long as you're not pestering Cade."

"I'm not pestering you, Cade. Am I?" Josh asked, crossing his arms defiantly.

Cade smirked. "Not at all. I like having a little buddy to help me do all the work."

He opened the door on the driver's side as Sarah and Josh climbed into the passenger's side, and he smiled at the picture. Years ago, he had dreamed of having a family with Sarah, but all of that had changed. He slid into the driver's seat and started his truck. It may be an impossible dream now, but he still had a chance to see what it would have felt like. If he were honest, he would have to admit it felt pretty good too.

"Are you excited, Josh?" Cade asked as he started up the truck.

Josh scoffed. "Not really."

"Well, don't picture it as having to go fill out paperwork. Think of it as a step towards being able to make some friends."

Josh shook his head. "I'm not good at making friends."

"What are you talking about? We're friends, right?" Cade countered, "And I'm excited to hear about all the new friends you'll make there."

"But what if I don't make any friends?" Josh countered.

"Oh, Honey," Sarah jumped in, "You'll make friends! You just wait and see!"

"That's what they said about my last school," Josh argued as he sunk down in his seat.

"Remember what I told you, Josh," Cade replied, "This is a new school and a new opportunity. It's not the same school where the kids picked on you. So, try to start fresh here. Forget about your old school and just see what adventures await you here."

Josh seemed to consider this before nodding.

"Alright, maybe I'll have at least one friend at some point to talk about."

"See? Isn't it better to think positive?" Cade asked, and Sarah laughed, shaking her head.

The rest of the drive to the school was pretty much like that, and Cade smiled to himself glad that Sarah had agreed to the trip. He really was enjoying himself, more so than he had in a long time, and it felt good. Since his accident, he had spent more time pushing people away than getting to know them, but with Sarah, things were different. He wanted to spend time with her and get to know her and Josh, even if his head repeatedly told him it was a bad idea, but without the rodeo coming between them, maybe there was a chance for them now. He couldn't shake that thought as they pulled into Josh's school, and Sarah and Josh got out. What if there was a shot things could work out this time? What if this could be their second chance? Would he take it? Would she?

As Sarah finished signing the last of the paperwork, the woman behind the desk smiled at her and stated, "Now, we don't normally do this, but since you're a friend of the Martins and this is a special circumstance, if you want to have Josh start today, that's totally fine."

"Today?!" Sarah exclaimed. She hadn't been expecting him to start school so soon. She had thought she would have at least a week or so with him before he had to go. This was happening so fast.

"Yes, Ma'am," the secretary stated with a smile and a nod.

"Oh, well, that's good...I guess, I was just thinking it would take longer to get him enrolled," she admitted.

The woman smiled sweetly and replied, "Well, it could have, but since Henry vouched for you two, we were able to expedite the process."

Sarah nodded, but she felt like someone had punched her in the gut. She wasn't ready to have to leave Josh behind. Not so soon. She hadn't mentally prepared for this! But as she turned around, she found him talking away with another boy his age. The two were happily talking about the video game character on Josh's shirt, and it appeared the other little boy's shirt boasted a different character from the same game. The two of them were smiling and laughing, and Sarah's heart warmed at the sight.

"Josh..." She hated to cut in, but it was

unavoidable.

"Yea?" He turned his focus to her.

"They said that you can start school here today if you want," she informed him, though she was hoping perhaps he would choose to wait.

"Really?!" he exclaimed, his eyes growing wide, "So, Alex and I can go to school together?!"

She smiled and nodded her head, and the two boys cheered and once more began their excited chatter.

"Now, Alex, please show Josh around to his classes," the secretary called, "And here are Josh's school books."

Sarah took them and started to hand them to her little boy, but as she did, she got down on his level and looked him right in the eye before asking, "Are you sure you want to stay? You don't have to, you know?"

"I'm sure, Aunt Sarah," he stated, throwing his arms around her neck and hugging her tight, "Thanks for making me go to school, and tell Cade he was right. I got a friend!"

With that, he ended the hug and took his books before hurrying off with Alex towards their next class.

Sarah's heart ached as she watched Josh walk down that hallway. He looked so small compared to this huge building, and she couldn't help feeling worried. As she turned to walk back outside, she prayed for him, because she knew even if she couldn't be with him today God would always be wherever he went.

She kept reminding herself of that all the way back to Cade's truck, and as she opened the door and started to climb in, Cade gave her a confused look and asked, "Where's Josh?"

"Apparently, they made an exception for him, and he was able to start today," she replied, "He decided he wanted to stay because he's already made a new friend."

Cade's face broke out in a big smile at that, and he stated, "I knew he'd make some friends here."

She nodded and gave him a small smile, before turning to look at the school once more. "Me too."

"Don't worry about him, Sarah." Cade's calm voice pierced through all her worries and brought her back to reality, but what she really noticed was the fact that he had placed his hand on her shoulder. She knew he had only meant it in a reassuring, comforting way, but it sent her skin tingling and made her oddly aware of his presence beside her. "He'll be fine. He's a tough kid."

She blinked, processing what he had said and forcing her mind to focus. She let out a deep breath and pulled her gaze away from the school. Cade was right. Josh would be okay. God had worked things out so far for them. She just had to trust Him that He would continue to do what was best for her and Josh.

"I know," she agreed, though she wasn't one hundred percent positive about it yet, "He's going to be fine."

When she turned around to face him, he quickly removed his hand, and she immediately felt the warmth disappear with it.

"That's the spirit!" Cade smiled at her and gave her a wink before putting the truck in gear and turning it in the direction of the repair shop.

She sighed, not sure what she had expected to happen. He had to take his hand back at some point. So, why did she feel so disappointed that he had? She turned back to face the school, praying for Josh once more and trying to ignore her feelings at this moment.

As they pulled out of the parking lot, Cade asked, "Did you ever think about what it would be like to be a parent?"

"What?" She whipped around to face him, wondering where that question had suddenly come from.

He shrugged, acting a bit sheepish. "It's just that

you became a mom so suddenly with your sister's accident and all," he clarified, "It had to have been hard to get adjusted to it."

She nodded, relieved that that was all he'd meant. "Well, it was in some ways, but I was always close to Stephanie so I felt like Josh's mom all of his life in some ways," she stated, immediately second guessing why she had said it like that!

He seemed to consider her words. "I guess that makes sense," he agreed with a nod, causing her shoulders to relax, "It's just that I can't imagine having a little kid thrust on you like that."

"Oh?" She felt her insides tense up. What was he trying to say? Don't get too attached? I don't want kids? What was he getting at?

"But you're doing a great job," he finished, surprising her, "I mean, Josh is a great kid, but he's lucky to have you. Not everyone would take in their nephew like you did and agree to raise him."

She smiled at that. "Well, it was an easy decision. He's family. There's no way I'm letting him ever go into that broken foster care system. Not if I can help it."

He nodded. "But even families don't always want the kid."

She frowned, her mind jumping back to when they were young. She had always wondered what his life had been like at home. She had never thought his dad had treated him very well, but she had never had any proof that he was abusive or anything. Was Cade talking about his own family or just making conversation?

"What do you mean?" she pressed him quietly.

He shrugged. "I don't know. I guess, some people have kids then blame them for how their life has turned out," he replied.

"Did your dad do that to you?"

He got quiet, his eyes solely focused on the road.

"I never asked before," she admitted, "I guess I should have, but I'd been afraid to."

He nodded. "It's okay. It's all in the past now. It doesn't matter."

She frowned, unsure of what to say next. Finally, she replied quietly, "I remember how hard it was on you when your mom died... I'm sorry that you had to go through that, Cade. I'm sure it was tough."

His eyes flooded with a sadness she hadn't seen since they were teenagers, and he shook his head, forcing a laugh. "How'd we get on such a serious topic as this, huh?"

She shrugged. "I don't know."

"Well, how about we change it to something better, huh?"

"To what?" she asked.

He thought on it; then, he smiled. "Are you liking being back on a ranch?"

She grinned and nodded her head. "Yea, I am. It's taking some getting used to, but I think it's going to turn out better than Josh and I had anticipated."

"Well, Josh certainly seems sold on the ranch," Cade joked, "I don't remember Stephanie liking horses that much. She always seemed to be too much of a girly girl to enjoy ranch life. I mean, she never seemed to want to get dirty and all that. Did her husband like horses as much as Josh does?"

Sarah shook her head. "Oh, no, he was allergic." Then, realizing what she had just said, she quickly added, "We always figured he got his love of horses from his grandpa."

"Yea, your dad did love his horses. He taught me a lot," Cade replied with a nod, but this time, he seemed to get lost in thought.

Her anxiety grew with each second he stayed quiet, and she worried about what he could be thinking.

Was he doing the math in his head? There wasn't much she could do to hide the timeline. Josh was nine going on ten after all. There was no way for her to hide that or change it. Her best bet at keeping her secret was to change the subject.

"How much farther to the repair shop?" she asked.

This seemed to pull Cade back into reality, and he smirked at her. "That eager to get rid of me, huh?"

"No," she stated quickly, "I was just wondering."

He nodded his head. "It's only a few more miles. We'll be pulling in soon."

"I hope the bill isn't too high," she worried aloud. "I really can't afford much right now."

"Don't worry about that," Cade replied, "The guys at the shop are really cool. They'll understand."

She considered that. "I've missed living in a small town. The big cities just don't have the same vibe. People don't look out for each other like they do around here."

He nodded. "Yea, when I was on the rodeo circuit, I saw all kinds of places, but none of them felt like home. Not until I found this little town with its diner from the fifties and the white church with the steeple where Henry preaches. Maybe it was 'cause everyone was so friendly or because it reminded me of life on your dad's ranch, but whatever it was, it just felt like I was finally home."

"You really loved my dad, didn't you?" she asked.

"He was the first man to act like a father to me," he replied with a shrug, "My old man loved the bottle more than anyone else, and to him, I was always just the thing that had held him back. Your dad was different though. He showed me how to ride and helped me learn all the secrets of how to train horses, and he was the first one to believe I could make it in the rodeo circuit. I'd wanted to make it too. I guess, I was hoping to make him proud."

"Is that why you locked your heels in about rodeo riding?" she asked the question but immediately wished she hadn't. She hadn't meant to bring up such a painful memory for both of them. They were having a good time. Now, she'd gone and spoiled it, and right after he had shared something about his past that he had never shared with her before. She frowned. Why did she always say the wrong things around him?

Just then, however, Cade pulled into the repair shop, and thankfully, one of the mechanics strode over to the truck, pulling Cade's attention away from her before either of them had to address what she had just said. She breathed a sigh of relief as she relaxed into her seat. That had been close. Why had she even asked that? She didn't want to dredge up the past...Did she? No, she wanted to move on and forget about it, to start over as friends and nothing more...Didn't she? Her frown deepened. Her head was beginning to throb. Why did things have to always be so complicated?

CHAPTER ELEVEN

Cade found it hard to concentrate as Miles talked to him. He tried. Oh, he tried! He wished he could just forget about Sarah's question, but it was wedged in his mind like a bone in a dog's mouth. He frowned. Why did he feel so uneasy about answering it? It shouldn't be hard. That was ten years ago, and a lot of time had passed. They had both grown and changed. In fact, things were actually going fairly well between them now, and strangely enough, he kind of hoped their friendship continued to grow. He had missed having her in his life, and yet thoughts of the breakup had stirred up a whole new set of emotions. He was enjoying spending time with her, but did he really want to risk the past repeating itself? Could he handle losing her again?

"Cade?" Miles asked, tilting his head as Cade was

suddenly pulled back into reality.

"I'm sorry. What?" Cade asked sheepishly.

"Dude, where are you? It's like you're a million miles away," Miles laughed.

Cade shook his head. "I don't know. I guess I got lost in thought. So, what were you saying?" Cade tried to dance around his question.

Miles smirked at him and nodded. "I was saying that one of the guys took her car out for a last minute test drive, but you two can come pick it up at one."

"One?" Sarah asked from beside him, "Why so late?"

"Well, it's almost noon now. By the time he gets back, everyone will be on their lunch break until one," Miles explained, "Sorry."

Before Sarah could say more, Cade cut in and stated, "That'll work. We'll just head over to the diner and get us some lunch while we wait."

"But what about lunch at the ranch?" she pressed, "I have to serve the chicken salad at noon."

"Just call Emmie and explain to her what happened," Cade informed her with a shrug, "I'm sure she'll be glad to do it. And if she can't, so what? Their lunch will be a little late. It'll be good for the ranch hands. It'll teach them patience."

"Or it could go the other way, and you'll have a riot on your hands," Miles interjected.

Cade shot him a look, and Miles laughed. "Okay, I get it. Not helping." He shook his head. "Sorry, one's the earliest I can have it ready for you."

"It's fine," she replied with a smile. "We'll make it work somehow."

With that settled, Cade put the car in reverse and waved goodbye to Miles and the rest of the crew. "We'll see you in a bit," he called.

"We'll be ready!" Miles responded.

As Cade turned back onto the main road and headed towards Andy's Diner, a popular lunch spot in town, Sarah shook her head beside him.

"It's okay. Everything'll work out," Cade offered, though he wondered what was really bothering her: the situation with her car or the question he had left unanswered?

She looked over at him for a second and nodded before turning her gaze out the window.

She had always liked to ride along with him when they were together before. Any time he was going anywhere, even before they were dating, she would ask if she could tag along, and they'd spend the whole trip talking. Well, in reality, he mostly just listened while she talked, but he still had enjoyed those times spent together. But this new found hesitation on Sarah's part only further convinced his heart that things had completely changed for the two of them. He waited for her to say something, but she didn't. He waited for several minutes, but they dragged on like hours. He shook his head.

"Okay, what's wrong?" he demanded.

"What?" she asked, blinking and turning to face him once more.

"You're never this quiet unless something's really bothering you," he informed her, "Most of the time, you're either laughing or yelling."

"Oh, how flattering..." She rolled her eyes.

"Hey, I just call it as I see it," Cade replied with a shrug, "But the only time you're quiet is when your afraid to speak your problems out loud. So, what's going on?"

She sighed and hung her head. "It's nothing. I was just wondering how Emmie will feel about me calling in like this."

He flashed her a smile. "Is that all?" he stated,

"Go ahead and call her. I'm sure it'll be fine."

She shook her head. "I wish I could have your confidence. I'm the newbie. I've only been working here a short time. I don't want them to get the wrong idea about me."

"It's fine, Sarah. I'm sure it will all work out. Just explain what happened to her, and I'm sure she'll understand."

She blew out a breath as her shoulders slumped. "Alright, I'm going to call her, but if you're wrong, you owe me a piece of pie."

"And if I'm right, you owe me the pie," he countered.

She smiled and nodded. "Agreed."

With that, she fished her cellphone out of her purse and gave Emmie a call.

After a few rings, Emmie answered, but all Cade could hear was Sarah's side of the conversation.

"Hi, Emmie," Sarah began, nervously playing with her hair, "I just called to ask a favor. My car isn't going to be ready to pick up until one o'clock, and the chicken salad for lunch is already made. So, I was wondering if you would be willing—"

Sarah's voice trailed off as Emmie apparently cut

in here.

"Are you sure?" Sarah asked, still sounding anxious.

Another long pause.

"Alright, thank you, Emmie." Sarah's voice was filled with relief as she continued, and Cade smiled to himself. He saw some pie in his future. "I appreciate it. I'm sorry about this. Thanks again."

Shortly thereafter, she hung up, and Cade gave her a knowing smirk.

"So, how did it go?"

She scoffed and playfully shoved his arm. "Don't rub it in! I'll buy you the pie!"

He laughed and nodded his head. "You'd better!"

It felt good to laugh and joke with Sarah again. He had missed this. He glanced at her out of the corner of his eye, watching her. She was sure beautiful when she laughed. He had almost forgotten what that looked like. He wished he could see this side of her more often.

Sarah glanced over at Cade as he pulled the truck into Andy's Diner's parking lot, and for a brief moment, she let herself wonder where their lives would have been had they not broken up that night before his rodeo show.

They probably would have gotten married. Cade would have known that Josh was his son. They would've had a house somewhere, probably on a ranch of their own, and they wouldn't have had all this tension between them whenever the past was mentioned.

But as she thought it over, she realized she wouldn't trade these past ten years either. Her faith had grown and was still growing, and Cade's obviously had too. They both weren't just Sunday Christians now. They each had their own relationship with God that they wouldn't trade for anything. They had grown so much. Maybe now, they would be able to have a more mature relationship. She frowned at that thought. Why was she thinking about their relationship? That was the last thing she needed to be thinking about right now.

"You coming?" Cade asked, causing her to blink, and she looked over to find him standing outside the truck and leaning on the door as he waited for her answer.

"Oh! Yea..." She nodded quickly, fumbling with the seat belt, "I'm coming."

She hurried after him, and he held the door for her as they headed inside. She smiled at him, as she tried to push her previous thoughts from her mind.

Once they were both sitting comfortably in a booth, a young pretty waitress came up to take their orders.

"Hi, Cade," she greeted sweetly.

"How's it going, Mary?" he asked, as he took two menus from her and handed one to Sarah.

"I'm just fine. How about you, Sugar?" she went on.

Sarah looked between the two of them. Were they dating? Had Cade purposefully brought her here just to tell her that he was in a relationship? She frowned. That didn't seem like Cade.

"We're doing fine. This is Sarah Makenna," he introduced her, "Sarah, this is Mary Alberts."

"It's nice to meet you," Sarah replied, but Mary made a slight face before catching herself.

"A pleasure I'm sure," Mary stated, but her words were laced with disdain.

Sarah smiled as she turned her focus on the menu. She remembered all the mean looks girls had given her for being Cade's girlfriend in high school. At the time, it had made her uncomfortable because she was afraid of all the competition. In truth, she figured it was because she'd thought maybe someday she might lose him that it

191

had bothered her so badly then. Now, she had lost him, and it was kind of fun being considered the competition for a change.

"So, how long have you known Cade?" Mary asked, pulling her away from the menu again.

"We go way back," she replied honestly, "We've known each other since middle school probably."

"Even before that," Cade corrected, "Remember, I poured punch all over your dress in the fourth grade at your cousin's birthday party."

"Oh-yeah!" She smiled wide at the memory, shaking her head and laughing. "I was so mad I could have killed you."

"And yet we became friends," Cade answered, leaning back in the booth with a smirk, "So, I must have done something right."

"As I recall, it wasn't you who had anything to do with it," she countered, "It was your grandma who made you apologize and give me a gift to make up for it."

"Yea, I gave you my slingshot!" His eyes suddenly held a wistful look as if he were reliving that day. "I forgot that I was there with my grandma." He shook his head. "Boy, I miss that slingshot!"

Sarah couldn't help but burst out laughing at his

over-dramatic tone.

"Oh-well, isn't this nice?" Mary cut in with an awkward laugh, "Remembering old times can be so fun, but you know what's more fun? Giving me your order."

Cade chuckled and smiled at her. "Yea, sorry, Mary," he replied. Then, glancing at his menu, he stated, "I'll take a cheeseburger with the works, some fries, Dr. Pepper, and a slice of your best pie." With that last order, he winked at Sarah and added, "That one's her treat."

"Lovely," Mary answered drolly, rolling her eyes subtly. Then, focusing her glare on Sarah, she asked, "And you?"

"I'll just have a salad and a sweet iced tea. Thanks."

"Oh, come on!" Cade objected, "This lunch is on me—all except the pie. So, go crazy. Get yourself something nice."

Smiling, she nodded. "Alright, I'll have the salad as a side, and I'll have—umm—the chicken sandwich, and sweet iced tea."

"And I'll get her a piece of pie too," Cade added.

Sarah shot him a look, and he smiled.

"Hey, I may have won the bet, but I can't eat pie in front of you like that. I mean, if I'm going to ingest all those calories, I don't want to be alone in that."

She chuckled and shook her head. "You're impossible."

"That it?" Mary demanded.

Cade nodded, handing her their menus. "Thanks, Mary."

She nodded, giving him a smile, and with that, she headed off to the kitchen to deliver their orders. However, as she did, she turned and shot Sarah another harsh look, and Sarah had to hold in a laugh. Didn't Mary realize there was nothing to be jealous of? Sarah and Cade were just friends. They could never be anymore. Not with their history.

"It's so weird how fast time flies," Cade stated, shaking his head, obviously oblivious to Mary's glare.

"What do you mean?" Sarah asked, glancing at her watch, "We've only been in here like ten minutes."

"Well, I was just thinking about that time that we met," he replied with a shrug, "My gramma had sure given me a talkin' to that day."

She laughed. "She was such a nice lady."

He nodded sadly. "She was."

"You know, even back then, I think your gramma wanted to see us end up together," she informed him, "I don't know why, but I just always got the feeling that she thought we'd make a good pair."

He laughed at that. "I'm sure she did," he replied, "She always liked you. She would have been heartbroken to see us break up. That's one thing I am glad she missed."

She nodded her head. "I guess she just didn't see how mismatched we were," she answered, though she wasn't even sure if she believed that.

He chortled. "Yea, I guess we just weren't meant to be."

Mary returned with a tray full of their food and drinks, before storming away without a word.

Once she was gone, Cade grabbed his cheeseburger and immediately started to eat, but Sarah watched Mary march out of the room. Believe it or not, she felt sorry for her. So, she leaned forward and whispered, "Don't you think you should go talk to her?"

"Why?" he asked after taking a swig of his pop.

"Well, she seems upset, and when I was your girlfriend, I—"

"Wait, you think Mary and I are—" He shook his head. "No way. She's a nice girl and all, but no."

"Oh..." Sarah blinked unsure of why she felt such

an incredible rush of relief wash through her body. Then, when she saw him smiling at her with that teasing look in his eyes, she shrugged, deciding to downplay it, and stated, "Well, it's too bad. I mean you would have made a cute couple."

"Maybe so, but she's a city slicker," he replied, "She hates the country. She's saving up to go to any big city she can find, and that's just not me. I like to live in the wide open fields."

"I remember," she stated, once again before she thought it over. She wished she would stop doing that!

He looked down at his fries thoughtfully and stated, "Yea, we used to know each other pretty well."

"That was a long time ago though," she countered, "Things have changed."

"Yea, they have," Cade agreed solemnly. Then, he cleared his throat and motioned to her. "I mean, look at you. You're a mom now."

That statement caught her so off guard she nearly dropped the sweet tea glass in her hand.

Cade gave her a teasing look and stated, "You always were clumsy. I'm glad to see some things haven't changed."

She smiled, grateful for the change in topic. "Yea,

I guess I was."

"I bet it was hard losing both of them so suddenly," he offered, his eyes getting wistful again, "I'm truly sorry about that."

She nodded, a fresh wave of sadness washing over her at the memories that flooded her brain. "It was, but I think they would have wanted to go together. They were inseparable in life, and they just got to go see Heaven together before the rest of us."

"Yea, but it's got to be tough on Josh too," he countered.

She sighed. "I think he tries not to think about it. That's part of why he didn't like school before. Everyone knew what had happened, and he couldn't pretend like everything was fine there."

Cade considered this and nodded. "I hope he'll like this school. I sort of feel responsible for him now that I talked him into going."

She smiled at the memory of listening to the two of them talking in the barn and nodded her head. "I'm sure he's having a great day. This is a wonderful town. Everyone's so nice. I bet his school will be the same."

She couldn't believe she was consoling him about Josh. She couldn't believe she was sitting here having lunch with him either! Last month if someone would have asked her where she would be right at this moment, she never in a million years would have guessed it would be sitting here with Cade Jacobs, and not only was she sitting with him, but she was also actually having a good time too!

Cade smiled at that and nodded. "Yea, you're right." Then, motioning to her food, he added, "You better hurry up and eat. Your food's getting cold, and one o'clock will be here before you know it."

She nodded and smiled, but suddenly a wave of guilt swept over her. Here she was eating lunch with Cade, and he had no idea what she had done to him...How she had hid his son from him all this time. He was being so kind, so friendly, so helpful, and all she had done was betray him, and he didn't even know it. At the time, she had just wanted to hurt him, like he had hurt her. So, she had kept Josh a secret, but now, she had forgiven him for running off to the rodeo. But would he be able to forgive her for never telling him he had a son? Would he be able to let those ten years she had robbed him of go?

Suddenly, her food didn't taste so good anymore, and she felt like she just needed to get out of here. She needed some air and some space. She couldn't look at Cade right now. Not when she was so confused.

"I've got to go get some air," she stated, abruptly rising and heading for the door.

"Uh—Okay..." She heard him say from behind her, but she didn't stop to look at him, for fear once she saw his face, her secret would spill right out of her mouth.

Cade sat there staring at their food with a frown as he leaned back in his chair. He supposed nostalgia had gotten a hold of him with Sarah here, and he had hoped they could enjoy things together like old times. But this wasn't old times. They had both changed, and she obviously found it still very hard to be around him. He had thought that maybe he and Sarah could start over, that they could at least be friends again, but that was clearly not what she wanted. He sighed as his shoulders slumped.

He pushed his pie away from him and turned to look out the window, suddenly not hungry anymore. He wasn't sure what he had expected to come out of this or what he had wanted, but it certainly wasn't supposed to go like this.

God, what was I thinking? he prayed silently.
*Lord, let Your will be done in all of this. I tried to
recapture a friendship from years ago, and it failed. I
don't know why You brought Sarah and I back together,
but help us figure out a way to be around each other
without hurting the other because right now I feel like
that's all we keep doing...*

With that, he stood and called to Mary that they
would be back. Then, he slipped outside to find Sarah,
wiping away tears from her eyes.

"Hey, now this isn't good," he stated softly, and
when she turned to face him, she just started to cry more.
He frowned and pulled her close to him, rubbing her
back and comforting her like he used to.

"What's the matter?" he whispered.

She shook her head, not saying anything, leaving
his mind to race through options of what it could be.

"Sarah," he began gently, "I'm sorry if I said
something that hurt you...I was really trying to let
bygones be bygones."

"Me too," she whispered.

"Then, why are you crying?" he pressed.

She swiped at her eyes and pushed away from
him as she regained her composure, and for a long

minute, he missed how she felt in his arms.

"I don't know," she informed him with a shrug, "I guess I just realized how much time we had wasted being angry with each other, and now, it's too late."

"Too late?" He blinked. "Too late for what?"

Her eyes widened, and she shook her head. "Nothing. It's just—" she hesitated before continuing, "What would your gramma think if she saw where we ended up?"

"Is that what has you all upset?" he asked, trying to stifle a laugh. "My gramma loved you. She would have said I was the biggest fool in the county for letting you slip away, and maybe I'd agree with her."

Her mouth dropped open. "What are you saying?"

"I wish I had fought harder for us," he admitted, "I shouldn't have run away when times got tough."

She shook her head. "Please, stop. We can't talk about this," she protested.

"Why not? I think it would be good for us to get some closure. Then, maybe we can build up something new, you know?" he pressed.

"Why do you always have to push?" she stated, shaking her head as she started to pace.

He studied her, feeling even more confused now.

"Sarah, what's wrong?"

"Nothing," she objected, "I just don't want to talk about something that's done and can't be changed. It'll only make us feel worse."

"But what if it brings some healing?" he pointed out.

"Since when do you want to talk about feelings?" she argued, "I seem to remember you hating any conversation that even remotely revolved around the topic."

"Well, that's before I saw you standing out here crying," he reasoned, "If I can help, I'd like to."

New tears welled in her eyes, and she shook her head in an effort to keep him from seeing them. "Oh, Cade, I wish you could," she admitted before rushing back into the restaurant and into the ladies' bathroom.

He shoved his hands in his pockets, wondering what was going on here. What was the matter with her? Then, it hit him. Maybe she was in some sort of trouble. He frowned. Then, why hadn't she said so? He sighed. Maybe he would talk all this over with Emmie. Maybe she would know what was going on because he sure didn't...

CHAPTER TWELVE

Cade climbed over the fence and entered Fantasma's corral once again. After his talk with Sarah outside Andy's diner, neither of them had had much of an appetite, and it was almost one anyway. So, they'd taken the rest of their food to go, and he'd driven her over to pick up her car. That had been the last he'd seen of her today. It seemed to him like she was avoiding him, but he wasn't sure why. He had tried to talk with her, but she hadn't engaged. So, he'd stopped trying, and now, he was just left wondering what had happened. He'd tried to talk with Emmie about it too, but she'd just gotten quiet as she listened. He had a feeling she had an idea of what was wrong, but when he'd tried to press her on it, she wouldn't let him in on her hunch. She'd just said she'd try talking with Sarah at some point, but he didn't see how that would do any good. Sarah had made it clear that she didn't want to talk about it...whatever it was. He just hated the thought that she was in trouble, and there was nothing he could do to help her. They may not be engaged anymore, but he still cared about her.

He shook his head as he realized he needed to focus on the job at hand, not on Sarah and her problems. He blew out a breath as he approached Fantasma slowly with a saddle blanket in his hand. He wanted to get her to trust people again, despite what her previous owners had done to her, and his hope was to someday get her saddle broken again. However, for today, he was willing to settle for her just letting him put the blanket on her back. He needed to get her used to these things again slowly. She was scared. She needed time. He understood all of that, but he needed to keep her moving forward too. That was his job after all.

She whinnied in protest and stuck her tail up in the air as she ran away from him. She was just like Sarah, running scared at the first sign of something different. He scowled, forcing his mind back on the task at hand. He couldn't afford to be distracted right now.

"Oh, come on, Girl," he offered gently, "It's not

that bad. This is just a blanket. You'll see. It'll be fine. Just trust me."

He tried approaching her again as he spoke, but she immediately darted to the other side of the corral. He blew out a breath and tried again. She was watching him. He knew she was curious about what he was doing even if she didn't want to be. She had grown to trust him slightly during their time together, and he had a feeling soon she would break down and let him near her.

Just then, he heard a car driving up the lane, kicking up dust as it did. His mind went straight to Sarah and Josh. They should be coming back from school now. He forced himself not to turn around and look at the car. He didn't want to see her, but in his heart, he wanted to turn around. He wanted to hope that she had come to her senses and calmed down. He shook his head and tried again to get the saddle blanket on Fantasma, but his motions were too abrupt and sudden. He spooked her again, and she zipped past him, nearly knocking him over in the process. He coughed and waved the dust from his face. Things between him and Sarah had changed. He had to remember that. He and Sarah had ended things years ago, and that was that! But if that were true, why did he feel so disappointed with how today had gone?

God, what am I doing? he prayed, turning his face towards Heaven, *I'm such a fool. I don't know what I've been hoping for, but things just aren't going well. I need to accept things as they are, not as what they were, but I'm going to need Your help with that.*

"Whatcha' doing?" a familiar voice asked from behind him.

He smiled at Josh and motioned to the saddle blanket. "I'm trying to get her to wear this."

"It doesn't look like she wants to," Josh pointed out.

"Yea, but that's just because she's scared," Cade informed him.

"What's she scared of?" Josh made a face. "It's just a blanket."

Cade smiled and chuckled slightly, hanging his head. "It might look like that to you, but to her, it's a reminder of some of the scary stuff she's gone through."

"A horse can get scared?" Josh asked wide-eyed.

Cade nodded. "Sure, everyone gets scared."

"Even you?" Josh sounded as though he didn't believe that, but Cade nodded, his voice quiet.

"Yea, even me," he informed him, but even as he

did, his mind suddenly jumped back to the day of his rodeo accident. Yea, he had been scared that day. Scared he may never walk again or may never live to see another day, but by the grace of God, he had. God had given him a second chance, and he had done his best not to waste it. He wondered. Could God be giving him a second chance with Sarah?

"When I grow up, I'm not going to be scared of anything!" Josh declared proudly, "Not even spiders."

"Oh-really?" Cade asked, raising up an eyebrow at him. He remembered the little boy already declaring he wasn't afraid of anything when they had first met, but he didn't call him on it. He just played along and let Josh talk big.

Josh nodded emphatically.

"How did school go?" Cade asked, changing the subject.

Josh shrugged. "Alright, I guess. It's still school, but no one pummeled me if that's what you mean. Plus, I made a new friend. His name is Alex, and he likes the same video games as me."

"That's good! See? I told you this school would be different," Cade replied, trying to look on the positive side.

Josh nodded. "Yea, I guess it was." Then, looking gravely serious, Josh asked, "Cade?"

"What's up, Buddy?" Cade turned around to face him.

"Can I try?" he asked.

"Try what?" Cade countered, tilting his head as he did to study the kid.

"Can I try talking to the horse?" Josh clarified.

"Oh, no..." Cade shook his head. "She's too wild."

"But if I just stay on this side of the fence, I'll be safe, won't I?"

"Yea, but—"

"Pleeeaaassseeee!" Josh begged.

"Alright, fine," Cade relented with a sigh, "But you have to stay on that side of the fence." He pointed to the spot where Josh was standing for emphasis. Sarah would kill him if Josh climbed into the corral with a wild horse. She might even kill him for letting him do this!

Josh nodded. "I will. I promise."

"Now, don't get your hopes up. She doesn't like anyone," Cade informed him as he climbed out of the corral to stand next to Josh. He handed him a sugar cub and stated, "But you can hold your hand over the fence and offer this to her. We'll see what she does."

Josh was beaming from ear to ear as he did just what Cade had said.

"Can I ride her when you teach me how to ride?" Josh pressed.

Cade shook his head and smiled. "No, I don't think that's such a good idea. She's not saddle broken yet."

"But I like her," Josh declared, and to Cade's amazement, he watched as Fantasma made her way across the corral to eat the sugar cubes from Josh's hand.

Josh giggled as the horse's tongue rubbed across his hand, and he stroked her neck as he offered her another sugar cube.

Cade's mouth was nearly hanging open as he watched the two of them. This kid was a natural with horses! He'd never seen anything like this!

Josh smiled wide as he looked over at Cade. "I think she likes me!"

Cade nodded. "I think she does too."

"Do you think you can teach me how to ride today?" Josh asked, and Cade nodded.

"Sarah said you could, didn't she?" he replied.

"Then, once I learn how to ride, can I ride her?" Josh asked, stroking her muzzle.

Cade frowned. "We'll see. Before that though, you both have to learn a lot."

"She has to learn stuff too?" Josh gave him a weird look, and Cade nodded.

"She has to learn to let people ride her again; otherwise, she's just going to buck you off."

"Oh, she wouldn't do that!" Josh informed him confidently.

"Well, just in case," Cade replied, "We'll take it slow. Now, if you're ready to learn how to ride, follow me."

"Alright!" Josh exclaimed. Then, patting her neck and giving her the last sugar cube, he turned his focus to Fantasma. "Sorry, Girl. I've got to go, but I'll be back."

And with that, he hurried towards the barn where all the other horses were, and Cade followed after him, still trying to wrap his mind around what had just happened here.

As she stood alone in the kitchen mixing up a fresh batch of hamburgers and fries, Sarah couldn't understand why she was feeling so guilty all of a sudden. She had lived with the secret about Josh for ten years, and never had it bothered her this badly. Usually, it only bothered her at night, keeping her wide awake all throughout the late hours, but in the morning, when life got busy, she was able to drown it out. Here though...Here, she couldn't seem to shake it. She was constantly reminded of her lie every time she looked at Cade's face, and he was trying so hard to be a better man and friend. She could tell, and that was driving her crazy! If he were cruel and nasty, it would be easy to keep punishing him, but she couldn't keep doing that, not when he was growing to once again be someone she cared about. She blinked at the admission as she flipped another hamburger. She was starting to care about Cade Jacobs again? She had never dreamed she would feel anything but anger towards him. When had all of this changed? She shook her head.

"Is there anything I can help you with?" a voice startled her out of her musings, and she jumped as she turned around to find Emmie staring at her.

Sarah smiled. "I'm alright. I don't want to bother you."

"Oh, it's no bother!" she exclaimed quickly, "After doing this for so many years, it's hard to quit cold turkey, you know what I mean?"

Sarah nodded. "Yea, I know what you mean."

"If you don't mind my asking though, is something wrong?" Emmie asked, giving her a concerned look, "This morning, you had seemed so happy, but now, you look troubled. Aren't you feeling well?"

"Oh, I'm fine," Sarah stated, trying to look much more chipper than she felt.

"I see..." Emmie studied her closely. Then, she walked over and started cutting up an onion. While she did that, she asked, "Cade told me about what happened at the diner. He's worried about you. He thinks you're in trouble."

Sarah looked over to face her, but the older woman's gaze was focused on the onions she was cutting. What could she say? What should she say?

"It was nothing," she replied with a shrug, "We were talking about old times, and I got emotional. Cade read too much into it."

"Ohh," Emmie replied with a nod, "Okay, well, I just hate to see anybody in pain. So, if something does come up or you change your mind, I'm here to talk, just in case maybe you could use a friend."

Sarah sighed and looked away. Her grip tightened on her spatula, and she wondered if maybe she might feel better if she did tell someone else the secret that was eating her up inside.

Suddenly, her hamburgers sizzling brought her attention back to the meal she was preparing. She started once more flipping them over and slapping cheese on half of them. That done, she turned to face Emmie, who had moved on to cutting up the lettuce.

"A lot has happened between Cade and me," she explained, "Maybe you've already guessed by my rude behavior to him that first night I was here, but things did not end well between us."

"What happened between you two?" Emmie pressed, finally looking up at her.

She blinked in surprise. "You mean, Cade never told you?"

Emmie shook her head. "This is probably no surprise to you, but he doesn't tend to share his feelings well."

Sarah scoffed at that. Oh, how she knew that. She took in a deep breath for courage. She'd never told anyone except her mom and sister about the breakup, and she hadn't talked about it for years. But somehow, she felt ready to stop holding on to it so tightly.

"My father was in the rodeo, and when Cade

started working at our ranch, my dad saw potential in him. He got him started in the rodeo too, and he was really good. Well, Cade and I also started dating around that time, though we had been friends since we were just young kids, and somewhere, along the way, we got engaged," Sarah explained, but her heart started to ache, knowing what she was going to have to say next. "Then, during a totally normal show, my father was doing his normal routine. Nothing out of the ordinary. All of a sudden, he was bucked off the bull he was riding and trampled to death." Tears sprang to her eyes, surprising Sarah. It had been years, and yet still the thought of that night tore her up inside like a cheese grader.

"Oh, my! That's terrible. That must have been so hard for you and your family," Emmie responded with sympathetic eyes, "I'm so sorry, Sarah."

"Well," she forced herself to continue with the tale, because she feared if she didn't, she was going to break down sobbing, "Cade still wanted to go and compete in his rodeo competition even after seeing what had happened to my dad, and I didn't want him to. I had seen what the rodeo could do, and I didn't want that to happen to anyone else I loved. So, I tried to force him not to go, but instead of listening to me and staying, he ran. He ran right to the rodeo and never looked back. Up until recently, I hadn't seen him since."

"And that was how many years ago?"

"Going on ten years this year," she replied.

"I see," Emmie nodded, "It must be hard seeing him again after all this time."

Sarah agreed. "It is, but we decided to call a truce and keep things civil."

"It seems to me Cade might be interested in keeping things more than civil," Emmie pointed out.

"Oh, no," Sarah quickly objected, though she couldn't deny that her heartbeat kicked up a notch at that, and she secretly wanted to know all of the details about why Emmie thought that Cade might like her again. Had Cade said something to her? "He's just trying to be friendly. That's all."

"Oh.." Emmie nodded thoughtfully. Then, giving Sarah a piercing look, she asked, "Is there a reason why you're afraid for it to be more than just a friendship? Is there something else bothering you?"

Sarah felt her heart freeze inside her chest. What reason did Emmie suspect? Had she figured it out?

Sarah felt so tired of keeping this secret. It felt like a weight that just kept dragging her deeper and deeper under water. Finally, she looked up with anxious eyes and asked, "Can I tell you something?"

"Of course."

"But you have to promise to keep it a secret!" Sarah pressed.

Emmie nodded, her face growing serious with concern. "What is it?"

"It's been so long since I told anyone this," Sarah began, "I don't know where to begin."

"How about at the beginning?" Emmie gently prodded.

"Well, after Cade left, I discovered I was pregnant." She hung her head before quickly adding, "I didn't know what to do, and I certainly wasn't going to call Cade up after everything we'd said to each other. Then, my sister had an idea. She had always wanted a child, but she and her husband weren't able to conceive. So, we went off on a trip together. I had Josh, and when we came back, we played it off like he was Stephanie's baby. Truth be told, I've regretted that decision ever since." Then, looking at the ground and swiping at a tear, she added, "But I can't change it now."

Emmie quickly crossed the kitchen and pulled Sarah into a hug. "It's never too late for a second chance, and I know it's not how you wanted it to be, but you're Josh's mom now."

"It's just so much harder living with this secret than I thought it would be," Sarah admitted.

"Because of Cade?" Emmie pressed.

Sarah looked away but nodded. "I never meant to hurt him, not really. I was just so angry, and I was scared. I didn't know what else to do. I guess I was afraid if I told him then I would never know if he chose me for me or for the baby."

"So, you kept it a secret all this time," Emmie replied, "I thought it was something like that."

"What?" Sarah asked, tilting her head.

"I wondered if it was something like that that was bothering you," Emmie explained, "I was figuring up Josh's age in my head, and I don't know." She shrugged. "It seemed coincidental, and to be honest, Josh is the spitting image of Cade. It's really remarkable." Then, taking a deep breath, Emmie asked, "So, are you going to tell Cade the truth now? I mean, with the three of you living here in such close proximity to each other, it's only a matter of time before he puts two and two together and figures it all out."

"But I can't tell him!" Sarah argued, "We're

getting along so well, and he won't understand. It'll ruin everything."

"Sweetheart, lying never solved anything," Emmie pointed out, "Besides, with the way you've looked all day, I'd say you're pretty miserable already. This lie is eating you up inside, and it's going to ruin your relationship if you let it."

"We don't have a relationship anymore. We can't..." Sarah shook her head.

"Maybe you could if you didn't let the past hold you back," Emmie countered, "I've seen how you two look at each other, and Josh adores him. What are you waiting for? You could do a lot worse than Cade Jacobs."

"I'm scared, Emmie," Sarah surprised herself by admitting that.

"Of what?"

"Scared that if I tell him the truth he won't want anything to do with me. Scared that he'll hate me. Scared that it'll end up hurting Josh in the end. Scared that I'll end up all alone," Sarah replied, the fears practically tumbling out of her mouth faster than she could say them.

"Well, my dear, I can understand that," Emmie

replied, "but sometimes we just have to leap and trust God with all our what if's and fears."

Sarah shook her head. "I don't know if I can do that."

"What do you feel like God is asking you to do?" Emmie challenged her. "If He's asking you to tell Cade, then you've got to do it. God will work things out between you two. It might be rough at first, but at least, you'll know you did what you were supposed to do."

"And what if I don't?" Sarah posed the question, "What if I just let things continue on like they are?"

"Then, I think you've got a lot more days feeling like you do right now in your future," Emmie replied.

Sarah sighed and shook her head. "It's just so hard."

"I know," Emmie agreed, placing a comforting hand on her back, "But just try trusting God. I think He'll surprise you."

Sarah nodded her head. "I'll pray about it," she finally relented.

Emmie gave her a smile and a pat on the back. "That's good. I'm sure you'll feel better after some time with the Lord, and I'm sorry if I overstepped or anything. It's just that I don't want you to let your fear hold you back. It could spoil everything."

Sarah frowned slightly. Even if she was letting fear hold her back, what else could she do? She wasn't sure she was brave enough to overcome this fear on her own. *Do you trust me?* The question entered her mind like a leaf on the breeze, and it caught her off guard. Did she trust God to work everything out even if Cade didn't take the news well? Did she trust Him to look after her and Josh no matter what was to come?

"Don't be sorry," Sarah replied, hugging the older woman, "I appreciate the advice. I really do, and it helped just to have someone else to talk about this with."

"That's alright, Honey," Emmie replied, giving her a smile. Then, clicking her tongue, she added, "Well, what else do you need me to fix while you're finishing the hamburgers?"

Sarah smiled, but on the inside, she still felt upset. *God, what am I to do? If I tell him, he'll hate me. Any chance of us being together will be ruined, but if I don't tell him and he finds out someday on his own, that'll be even worse. What do I do?*

Do you trust me? The question popped into her mind again, and her shoulders slumped. She knew what God wanted her to do, even if it did terrify her, but could she do it? She'd at least told Emmie her secret. She'd finally been able to share it with someone other than her sister, and it had gone well. Maybe she could handle telling Cade.

However, she had a feeling telling it to Cade was going to be an entirely different ballgame. What would he think of this news? How would he react? They had only been around each other for a few weeks now, and she didn't think that their relationship could survive this type of deception. She couldn't tell him...Could she? She frowned as she sent Emmie over to cut up the tomatoes. She knew she was supposed to trust God, but she was still scared. All of this uncertainty was enough to drive her crazy!

CHAPTER THIRTEEN

"Alright," Cade began as he motioned in front of him as he spoke, "Here's your horse!"

Josh's eyes widened with glee as he approached the buckskin quarter horse Cade had picked out for him.

"Is it really my horse?" Josh asked, gently reaching up to stroke his nose.

Cade smiled, watching the two contentedly, and he stated, "Sort of. It's like you're renting him. He's still technically Henry's, but he's all yours to ride."

Josh's smile grew, and he asked, "What's his name?"

"McLintock," Cade replied.

"McLin—What?" Josh shot him a funny face, and Cade laughed.

"He's named after a John Wayne character," Cade explained, "But you can call him Mick."

"Mick! Okay," Josh replied with a nod, "I can do that."

"Alright, so first thing you're going to want to do is mount up," Cade declared.

However, as Josh started to do just that, Cade stopped him.

"Uh-uh-uh, you don't get on from this side. All cowboys get on from the left side," Cade informed him.

"Why?" Josh asked.

"It's got to do with your tack and gear."

"Oh, okay," Josh replied with a shrug as he moved to the other side.

"Alright, now to mount your horse," Cade informed him, "Put your foot in that stirrup and grab the saddle horn. Then, pull yourself up and throw you right leg over the top, and the momentum will carry you over."

Josh tried a few times before he managed to pull himself up, but once he had, he sat proudly atop his horse. He looked over at Cade and asked, "What's next?"

"Grab your reigns, give them a snap, and kick in your heels," he replied, "And make a clicking noise with your mouth. That'll tell your horse you want to start heading out. Just always be gentle at first."

Josh nodded and tried his best to mimic what Cade had said. After Cade gave him a few more pointers, he was doing well, and Cade made sure to cover how to stop the horse and how to control him with the reins. Josh was beaming from ear to ear, and as Cade had suspected, he was a natural. It seemed horse riding was in his DNA, and it didn't seem to intimidate or scare him like it did other newbies. He smiled to himself. If only Sarah could see him now...He frowned, wondering where she was. After all her worries about Josh riding, he was surprised she hadn't shown up to supervise the lesson. Then again, she had been seemingly avoiding him since lunch. He frowned. That woman was so hard to read, and yet he couldn't help himself. He was fascinated by her, and he loved watching her with Josh. This was a new side of her that he had never gotten a chance to see, and he realized she would have made a great mom. Just as his mind started to wonder to what their lives would have been like had they not broken up that night ten years ago, he heard someone clear their throat behind him.

"Cade, we need to talk."

He stiffened immediately at the seriousness of Sarah's tone. What had he done now? He slowly turned his attention from where Josh was still practicing trotting. She looked so pretty with her hair done up in a loose ponytail and her gingham apron over her white shirt. In fact, she didn't look angry at all. Actually, she looked more worried than anything. Maybe he wasn't the one in trouble.

"What's up?" he asked, quirking an eyebrow up at her.

She shook her head. "Josh, go wash up for supper, alright?" she called over to him.

"Ah-man," Josh whined.

Seeing how serious her eyes were, Cade added, "Don't worry about unsaddling your horse. I'll handle that."

"Alright, thanks, Cade," Josh relented as he slid down and headed off to wash up.

Once he was gone, Sarah took in a deep breath, and Cade braced for what was about to come. He had a feeling it wasn't good, whatever it was.

"I'm sorry about earlier," she stated, and he immediately relaxed. Was that what all this fuss was about?

He chuckled. "It's cool, Sarah. Don't worry about it."

"No, let me finish," she pressed on, and he frowned. So, there was more.

"I—um—was so upset before, because I was really having a good time with you," she admitted, and he smiled.

"That doesn't seem like a reason to cry," he pointed out.

"Well, it just made what I've been doing torturous because I don't want to hurt you, but I also knew I couldn't talk to you about it without it affecting our relationship. In fact, it'll probably never be the same again. But after talking with someone, I know God wouldn't want us living this way, and I realized that you'd probably figure out the truth on your own anyway. So, it'd be better for me to tell you now than for you to learn about it some other way later, right?"

He blinked, feeling confused. "I guess so. I'm not sure what we're talking about here though."

She let out a deep breath slowly and shook her head. "I can't believe I'm going to do this. I promised myself I never would."

He wasn't liking the sound of all of this, and he

shook his head. "Hey, Sarah, don't worry about it. We can talk later. Right now, you ought to be getting ready for the supper rush."

She nodded. "I know." Glancing at her watch, she added, "I've got a little more time before I have to serve everything, and the food's all done, just warming. But I need to get this out. If I don't now, I might never have the courage to do it again."

Crossing his arms, he tried to mentally prepare himself for whatever she had to say.

"Alright, go ahead," he stated with a nod.

"First off, let me say when we broke up before, I was angry. I was hurt that you chose the rodeo over me, and I didn't want to win you back by anything other than your love for me."

"I didn't choose the rodeo over—" His voice trailed off as memories of that time flooded back to his mind, and he realized how maybe she could have viewed it that way.

"Well, when I—After I realized we were not getting back together—" She shook her head. "Why is this so hard?"

"Spit it out, Sarah. I can take it," he offered, feeling apprehensive to hear what it was though.

"Josh is—Josh isn't my nephew," she blurted out, "He's my son."

Cade's eyes widened, and he took a step back, leaning against the railing of the coral. If Sarah was his mom, then that meant—

"You're his father, Cade," she finished, looking down at the ground, "I didn't know about it until after we had broken up, and I didn't want you to come back to me because of a baby. And I was hurt. So, I kept him a secret, and my sister raised him like her own. They had never been able to have kids of their own, and I thought it was the best solution for all involved."

His temper flared at that, and he demanded, "But what about me?! I didn't even get a choice in the matter!"

She shook her head. "You were an up-n-coming rodeo star. What would you have done with an infant?"

"I don't know," he snapped, crossing his arms, "But it would have been nice to have had the option."

"Well, things don't always work out the way we want them too!" she shot back, "At the time, I had dreamed of us being married and living in a big white house all of our own, and that didn't happen."

"What? Just because I went to the rodeo? Lots of

people have families and ride the circuit. Even your dad did it!" he argued.

"You weren't just going to the rodeo. You were running away," she countered. "Things were getting hard between us, and rather than dealing with it, you ran off to the one place I had told you not to."

He shook his head as he started to pace. He needed to move, to do something; otherwise, he was going to explode.

"You were always trying to control me, telling me what I could do and couldn't do! Then, when I didn't do what you wanted, you took my son from me!"

"Cade, it wasn't like that," she offered, but he was done listening.

"I can't believe I had—" Cade stopped short of admitting what he had let himself start feeling again. He shook his head.

"I'm sorry, Cade. I was young. I was scared. I was hurt. I didn't know what to do."

He stopped pacing and turned around to face her. "I understand all of that, but for all this time when we've been working together, when you've been watching Josh and I, when we've been hanging out again, when I thought we were—" He shook his head. "All of this time, you've been lying right to my face."

Tears welled up in her eyes as she reached out to touch his arm, but he backed away from her. "I didn't know what to do. It had been such a shock seeing you again, and then when we started bonding again, rebuilding our relationship, I was afraid of ruining that. I hadn't realized just how much I had missed you," she admitted, "I was afraid, if you knew the truth, you would hate me."

"All this time..." He shook his head, still trying to wrap his mind around it all. "You've had all this time to tell me the truth, and you tell me now. Why? Why now, Sarah?"

"Because I—" She stopped herself short and swiped the tears from her eyes. "I couldn't go on keeping it a secret from you. It was eating me up inside."

He scoffed. "Someone else knows, don't they?" he demanded.

"What?"

"You said you talked with someone," he pressed, "That's why you're telling me now because you're afraid that they'll tell me instead."

She shook her head. "No, it's not that at all. Yes, I did talk with Emmie, and she said I should tell you the truth. But I didn't tell you just because I was afraid she would. I'm telling you because I thought it was what God would want me to do."

"It's a little late to be thinking about God, don't you think?" he shot back, but he regretted his words as he watched the hurt wash over her face.

She paused for a long time, looking at the ground. "I'm sorry, Cade," she finally stated, "I really have been enjoying our time together again. I don't think I ever truly stopped—" Her voice trailed off, and she shook her head. "I—I have to go. It's time to dish out the meal."

He nodded, crossing his arms. "What's stopping you?"

She opened her mouth as if to say something, but she just as quickly shut it and walked away, hanging her head and swiping at her eyes.

Cade began to pace again before punching the corral fence behind him. Josh was his son? He was a dad?! All this time...He had lost all this time with his son. He had promised himself that when he had kids he was going to be a better father than his dad was, but now look at him! At least, his dad had been around even if he had been a drunk! Cade had missed so many milestones with Josh, and he hadn't even had a chance to try. He had been robbed of his chance, but what hurt worse was knowing Sarah had been able to look him in the eye all this time and let him believe her lie. She had lied to him. She was a liar, just like his old man. He couldn't believe he had almost let himself fall for her again. What a mistake that would have been! He shook his head as his chest ached inside of him. He felt like his world had just gotten toppled over, and there wasn't anything he could do about it. He sighed as he climbed over the corral and headed over to unsaddle McLintock. What else could he do? What else did he want to do?

As Sarah dished up the supper for all the ranch hands, she tried her best to hold her emotions in check, and yet still worry nagged at her. Cade hadn't taken the news well. He had been much angrier than she had expected. What if he tried to fight her for custody of Josh? Then, poor little Josh's world would be turned upside down. He would learn the truth, and everything he had ever known would seem like a lie. She might even lose him, and she couldn't imagine a world without Josh anymore. She frowned as she realized she had begun to feel that same way about Cade. It had been so nice having him back in her life again. He was so sweet, kind, and considerate. She had hoped somehow that they could continue to have that kind of relationship even after she'd told him the truth, but she had known it in her heart that they couldn't. Her lie had been too big, too painful. Once it was revealed, it was like an atomic bomb. It just destroyed their relationship and didn't even leave a sliver behind. She hung her head as she served up the food to each passing plate, but pretty soon, Josh came running in and stood beside her.

"Did you see me on my horse, Aunt Sarah? Did you? Did you?" he asked, nearly bouncing up and down.

"I did," she replied, trying to keep her tone light, "You were doing a great job."

"Thanks," Josh stated proudly, "Cade told me I was a natural."

"I bet you are," she agreed, new tears welling in her eyes, "You like Cade a lot, don't you?"

He nodded. "Yea, he's pretty cool."

She quickly swiped away the tears in her eyes before Josh could see them and stated, "You better get your supper now before it runs out."

"It won't run out, Aunt Sarah," Josh chided her teasingly, "You always make sure to make plenty!"

She smiled at the compliment, but she still needed

him to leave before he saw through her brave front. "Go on now."

"Okay," he replied as he started to walk off, but just as quickly, he doubled back and threw his arms around her, hugging her tightly. "Thanks, Aunt Sarah, for letting me ride horses today. You're the best aunt ever!"

Now, the tears could not be held back, and she began to sob.

"What's the matter, Aunt Sarah?" he asked, gently touching her face.

"It's nothing," she replied, dismissing him with a wave. "It's just that that was really sweet of you to say."

"So, I made you cry?" he asked, making a face, "Because I was sweet?"

She laughed, wiping her cheeks off and trying to feign confidence. "It's a lady thing. Your wife will do this too someday."

Josh stuck out his tongue and shook his head. "Boy, I hope not."

She smiled and patted him on the back. "Now, go on and get your supper."

"Are you sure you're okay?" he pressed, his eyes searching hers.

Apparently, her act hadn't been as convincing as she would have hoped.

"I'm fine," she informed him with a nod of her head.

He smiled, satisfied with that. "Alright, I'll go get something to eat then."

"Good," she replied with a smile of her own.

With Josh taken care of, she went back to work, but she noticed a distinct lack of one certain cowpoke as she went about serving the rest of the line. Cade hadn't shown up yet...Not that she had really expected him to, but in her heart, she had hoped to see him there. Oh, how she wished to hear him say everything was okay now. That he had forgiven her and wanted to move on from the past...That he loved her in spite of everything just as much as she loved him. She swiped at a rebellious tear that trickled down her face. But she was only playing make believe. He wasn't here. He wasn't going to come. She had ruined any second chance she had hoped to get with him, and maybe it was for the best. She and Cade just weren't right for each other. Whenever they tried to build any sort of relationship together, it always ended like this. She might as well just face facts and accept it. But no matter how hard she tried to convince herself otherwise, she still felt like bawling her eyes out.

"So, Josh is your son?" Henry let out a low whistle and shook his head. "That must've thrown you for a loop, huh?"

"I feel like I got thrown from a bucking horse and trampled for my trouble," Cade agreed, resting his arms on the corral fence as he watched the sunset in the distance.

"So, what are you going to do?" Henry asked.

"What do you mean?"

Henry propped himself up on the fence next to Cade. "What are you going to do about Sarah and Josh?"

Cade blew out a breath and shook his head as he pushed himself off the fence and started to pace.

"I don't know. I just need some time to think, I guess," Cade declared, "It's a lot to take in, finding out you have a son you never knew about."

Henry nodded. "I can imagine."

"Plus, it's even harder to believe this sweet girl, who you thought would never even hurt a fly, has been bold-faced lying to you," he added. Then, hanging his head, he blew out a breath and perched on the fence again. "I thought maybe we were going to get a second

236

chance. Pretty stupid of me, right?"

"No, Cade, not stupid." Henry chuckled shaking his head. "Just naive."

Cade quirked up a brow as he stared at him.

"I just mean this whole situation was a lot more complicated than you bargained for," Henry explained. "You thought you were just trying to light some old flames, but now, you've got to deal with old buried secrets too. It's a lot to take in."

"What would you do, Henry? If it were you in my shoes?" Cade asked.

Henry considered this and nodded his head as if to reaffirm his decision to himself. "Oh, I'd do an awful lot of praying...And I mean a lot...Then, I'd talk to her about it. After all, you two are his parents like it or not. You're going to have to learn to communicate with each other."

"Communicate?! With her?!" Cade scoffed. "Every time we try to communicate, we end up in a fight."

"That may be so, but you're going to have to talk to her at some point," Henry pointed out, "Unless, you don't want to claim your paternal rights with Josh."

"I want to...I mean, I think I do..." Cade shook his

head and ran his hands through his hair. "Oh, I don't know. I don't know what to do! Things were so much simpler when I was alone on the rodeo circuit. I didn't have secret kids and past loves showing up at my door!"

"Well, I know some fellas in the rodeo circuit, who've had that very thing happen to them," Henry teased.

Cade shot him an unamused look. "This is serious."

"I know that, but you know what they say, 'Laughter is the best medicine' and 'It's healing for the soul,'" Henry replied.

Cade sighed. "Well, tonight, I don't feel much like laughing."

Henry nodded and placed a hand on his shoulder. "I know, Cade, but remember what I said. Pray...It's getting late, and the dark always makes things worse than they are. Tomorrow, you'll see things much clearer."

Cade nodded. "I hope you're right."

"I know I am. Remember, I'm a pastor too. This isn't my first rodeo," Henry winked at him, "Now, go get some sleep and don't worry about this. It'll all work itself out."

"But what if I'm not good at being a dad?" Cade asked quietly, more to himself than Henry. "What if I end up being like my father?"

Henry shook his head. "If you believe that of yourself, you're crazy. You'll be a great dad. Anyone who handles horses like you would have to be, and that kid's a great kid." Then, his tone getting more serious, Henry added, "Look. God gave you a second chance here. You may not have been a part of this kid's life before, but you have a chance to fix that. It's all up to you now. Everything depends on how you handle this."

Cade sighed, looking up at the stars that were starting to litter the nighttime sky.

"You make it sound so easy."

"That's because it is when you get right down to it," Henry explained, "But it's all our feelings, our pain, our heartache, and our hurt that complicates everything and makes it much more difficult to deal with."

Cade smirked at that. "I guess you're right."

"Well, I've been known to be so on a few occasions," Henry joked, "Now, I think I'll turn in and let you get to praying. You going to be okay?"

Cade nodded, smiling at his friend's concern. "Yea, I'll be fine, Henry. Thanks, and goodnight."

Henry returned his smile as he pushed himself off the fence with a moan. "Goodnight. Don't stay up too late. We've got an early morning tomorrow."

"We've always got an early morning," Cade replied.

"Yea, but it gets even earlier with the later you stay up," Henry reminded him.

Cade chuckled at that. "That is true."

Then, with a wave, Henry bid him goodnight once more before heading home. Cade watched him as he walked away, and he felt a pang of guilt. Henry was right. He should be praying right now. It should have been the first thing he did, but he hadn't. Why? He wasn't sure. Maybe, he blamed God for all this mess. He wasn't sure, but he knew the only one who could help him make any sense of this mess was God. So, angry or not, he did need to start praying. He just had to trust that God had had a reason for all this chaos, even if he didn't understand it.

He frowned as he headed towards his cabin. But how could all of this work out? Sarah had lied to him...Right to his face. She was no better than his father, and what about Cade? Was he really cut out to be a dad? He didn't want to mess up and make Josh's life miserable. Then, it struck him. Maybe why he hadn't prayed was because he was afraid of God's answer. What if God wanted them to be a family? Could Cade handle being a loving husband and a caring father? Could he handle the responsibilities day in and day out? What if he failed? What if he hurt them? Yes, he was afraid, he realized as he stepped into his cabin. He walked over to the sink to get a drink of water, but he didn't drink it. He just sat the glass down in the sink and leaned up against the counter.

"Oh, God, what am I supposed to do?" he prayed aloud.

CHAPTER FOURTEEN

"Aunt Sarah," Josh asked as he came into the kitchen where she was working the next day, "Why isn't Cade going to teach me how to ride horses anymore?"

"What?!" Sarah exclaimed, spinning around to face him, the suds from where she had been washing dishes still clinging to her hands, "What do you mean?"

"Well, I went to ask him if he wanted to give me my lesson after school, but he said I was going to have to get someone else to teach me," Josh replied, dragging his finger around the counter, "He seemed like he was upset 'bout something. Do you think I did something wrong?"

"No," she reassured him, clearing the distance between them in an instant and kissing the top of his head as she pulled him close. "Cade's upset with me, not you. Don't worry. I'll go talk with him and get this straightened out."

Josh frowned and crossed his arms. "Why is he upset with you?"

She looked away and hesitated. How could she explain this to him?

"Remember how I said we used to be friends a long time ago?" she asked him, and once he nodded, she continued, "Well, we used to be more than that. We almost got married."

"You and Cade!?" he exclaimed.

She nodded her head emphatically. "And sometimes, when people used to be that close, they just argue."

He agreed, but he still looked concerned. "Do you think that, once you're done arguing, he'll teach me how to ride horses again? I don't really want another teacher, Aunt Sarah."

"Don't worry. He'll be you teacher. He's just upset right now. Just give me some time to work it out," she replied confidently. Then, as she headed for the door, she called back over her shoulder to him. "Why not you work on your homework that way you're ready when it's time for your lesson?"

243

"Okay," he replied, setting his backpack down on the table.

Sarah wiped the suds off her hands as she marched down to the barn where it seemed she always found Cade, but he wasn't there. She frowned and crossed her arms. Now, where was he?

It was then that she saw Matt, the young ranch hand from before, coming out of the tack room with a bit and bridle in his hands.

"Matt, where's Cade?" she asked.

He nearly jumped out of his skin. He must not have been expecting to find anyone in the barn with him. She blushed and stifled a laugh, not wanting to embarrass him even more.

"He's—um—Up in his cabin," Matt explained hesitantly.

"Where's that at?" she pressed.

"If you just follow that path until it goes up the hill and into the trees, it'll lead you right to where his cabin is," Matt informed her.

"Thanks," she declared, turning on her heel and storming up the path before Matt could say anymore.

Once she got a hold of Cade, she was going to give him an earful! What was he thinking canceling horse riding lessons with Josh?! Of all the stupid, selfish...

She rounded the corner around a tree and found Cade's truck parked outside of his cabin. He was standing beside it as he put something into the bed of the truck.

"Cade!" she shouted as she cleared the distance between them in record time, "What's the big idea?!"

"Josh told you..." He hung his head and sighed.

"Of course he told me!" she snapped, "Why would you cancel his horse riding lessons?! He thinks he did something wrong! What's the matter with you!?"

He looked away and frowned. "I've been thinking about this whole thing, Sarah, and I just realized I couldn't live a lie like that. If I'm a father now, then I want to be his dad. I want to teach him things. I want to play catch. I want him to know who I am."

"But I can't tell him who you are without ruining everything. His whole little world will get upended. His parents just died. Do you really want to do that to him?!"

"No." He shook his head simply. "I've been thinking about this all night, and I know you don't want Josh to know the truth now. I know it's complicated, perhaps too complicated for a kid to understand, but that doesn't mean I can continue telling the lie."

"What do you mean?" she asked, some of the fire leaving her. He was calm, too calm. Last night, he'd been furious with her; now, he was just matter-of-fact. Something was wrong.

"That's why I stopped the horse riding lessons," he explained, "I can't stand to keep seeing Josh and not being able to tell him the truth. I can't lie to him."

"I'm not asking you to lie!" she snapped, "I just don't want you to tell him something that will hurt him!"

He shrugged, fiddling with something in the back of his truck. "It still feels like lying to me, and I'm sorry, Sarah, but I just can't do that."

"So, what are you going to do?"

"I'm going to leave," he replied, turning from his truck and heading for his cabin. It was then she stood on her tiptoes and snuck a peak at what was in the back of his truck. Boxes...Boxes of his personal belongings.

"Cade, what are you thinking?! You can't leave!" she snapped, storming after him, that fire inside her heating up again. "You have a job here!"

"Yes, but so do you, and you seem to need this job more than me," he informed her, "Besides, I got an offer to compete in another rodeo show, and I'm going to take it."

"Are you insane!? After what happened with your last rodeo accident?! You could've been killed! In fact, you almost died!"

He shrugged. "But I didn't."

"Cade, I won't let you go," she stated, stomping her foot, "This is madness. You're going to get yourself killed!"

"Well, that's just it, Sarah, you can't control me. It's my life to do with as I please," he replied.

"Of all the pigheaded stunts!"

"And what would you have me do?!" he snapped, his temper finally showing itself. "Just hang out here and pretend everything is alright?! Pretend like Josh isn't my son. Pretend like you didn't—That I don't still—" He shook his head. "You want me to live a big lie! I just can't do that!"

"But going back to the rodeo of all things! After your last accident, I would've thought you'd have learned your lesson!"

"I'd rather be dead than live a lie," he ground out the words, and Sarah froze.

"You don't really mean that," she countered.

He shrugged. "So, what if I do?"

"Everyone here loves you. You've got a good job. Don't throw it all away for nothing," she argued, "Josh and I will leave. I've saved up enough to get us to our next stop."

"No, Sarah," he countered, shaking his head, "This is my decision, not yours. I'm not going to change my mind. I've already talked it all over with Henry this morning. I'm leaving."

"Cade, what's it going to take to get through to you!?" she demanded, "I don't want you to go! I—I—I love you, okay?" She couldn't believe she had let herself actually say those words again after all these years. But she'd done it, and she'd meant every word of it too, she suddenly realized. "I'm sorry. This is all my fault. Don't do this."

He smirked at her. "It's too late, Sarah. My mind's already made up."

"Then, change your mind!" she argued, "This is suicide!"

"Well, thanks for the vote of confidence in my riding skills," he scoffed.

"You know what I mean!" she snapped, "I watched that last ride of yours on TV. I heard what they were saying. You're lucky to still be alive, and I've been reading up on the toll head injuries play on the riders too! There's no telling what head injury will be your last, or when you'll push it just a little too far. Cade, you're gambling with your life!"

"It's mine to gamble with if I want!" he snapped, turning around to face her, "I don't need you coming out here to tell me what to do! You always were like that. You had to control every little thing!"

"And you were always so pigheaded!" she countered, "You never listened to anyone else once your mind was made up!"

"If you had your way, I'd be a doormat!"

"If I had my way, you'd be alive and safe!"

"I'm alive now!" he argued.

"For how much longer?!" she countered.

He scowled and looked away. She frowned. Nothing seemed to be getting through to him. She had to try something else. Anything. She had to keep him from leaving. She just couldn't lose him again... Even though she had a feeling she already had.

"Cade, don't do this to Josh. He cares so much about you," she replied, "Please... Maybe when he's older, we can tell him the truth about us and him, but I just can't do it now, not after he just lost his parents. But please don't hurt him by leaving. It's my fault your angry. Take it out on me, but please, don't hurt Josh."

He frowned at her. "It's not going to work, Sarah. I'm not changing my mind no matter what you say. I'm leaving, and that's that. I can't live a lie, and I can't be around someone who could either."

"Do you think any of this was easy for me?!" She shook her head and moved her arms for emphasis. "The truth tore me up a little bit more each time I saw you! It was the hardest thing I ever had to do, but I did it for Josh."

"You did it for yourself!" he countered.

She looked away. "It's true that at the start it was for me, but since then, it's changed. There have been so many times where I wanted to tell Josh the truth too," she admitted, "But I couldn't. I knew what it would do to his world. So, I've kept it a secret until now. But the closer you and I became, the harder it was to tell you the truth and the harder it was to stay silent. I was caught up, and I didn't know what to do."

He started to pace and shook his head. "I don't care about your reasoning, Sarah. A lie is still a lie, and I'm not going to live like that!"

"So, instead, you're just going to run like you did

before?!" she snapped.

He shrugged. "I guess if that's what you want to call it."

"Well, fine then! Go! See if I care!" she shouted, her temper flaring, "You think you know it all, don't you?! But while you're out there killing yourself, just remember there's a little kid here that you're breaking the heart of!"

He frowned and looked away. "You can explain it to Josh in a way that he'll understand," he replied, "You're good at making up lies."

That tore it, and with a huff, she turned on her heel and stormed back down the way she had come. She couldn't believe she had ever let herself fall for such a stubborn, unreasonable man as Cade Jacobs!

Slamming down another box into the bed of his truck, Cade blew out an exasperated breath and ran a hand through his hair. Why did Sarah always have to make things so difficult?! He'd had made a plan. He had known what he was going to do. Then, she had come along and made things so complicated. He wasn't going to change his mind now though. She was just trying to make his mind up for him. She was still trying to control him, to get him to do what she wanted with little concern for what he wanted to do or why, but he had had enough of that sort of life growing up with his dad. He wasn't going to let anyone else control him ever again!

However, as he turned around to grab another box, he lost some of his anger and, with it, some of his steam. He didn't really want to have to leave. He enjoyed his life here, but yet, he wasn't sure he could handle living with lies. This job was becoming much too complicated. Whereas, the rodeo was never complicated. It was always straight forward. Just stay on the horse until you couldn't anymore.

He grabbed another box and once more headed outside.

Sarah just didn't understand. She didn't know how hard this was. She had been living with this lie since Josh was born. He was new to all of this, and he didn't want to get used to lying. His dad had been a bitter, controlling alcoholic, who'd told so many lies he forgot what the truth even was, and Cade had promised himself that he would never end up like him.

Cade frowned as he thought of Josh, but he quickly dismissed it. Josh would be fine. He had Sarah, and he had all the ranch hands and Henry who could teach him how to ride and show him the ropes around here. Cade's heart ached a little at the thought of Josh learning all this ranching stuff without him. Years ago, he had daydreamed about what it would be like to teach his kids everything he knew about ranching. He had always looked forward to seeing their eyes light up with joy as they learned about horses and the ranch. He shook his head as he put this box with the others. But Josh wasn't his son, not, at least, in a way he could claim. Sarah had made that clear. He couldn't lay any claim to his son. He had to just treat him like the nephew of a friend. Sadly, that wasn't the same. That wasn't what he had hoped it would be like.

Maybe he was just being stubborn. Maybe he was just being difficult. But he was sure of one thing. This was the right decision for him. He couldn't live with lies. He just couldn't, and if that meant going back to the rodeo, then so be it. Maybe this time, things would be different.

He blew out a breath and tried to steady his mind. His thoughts were all over the place along with his emotions. He wouldn't have thought one conversation with Sarah could do that to a man, but it could, at least to him. He supposed the hardest thing about all of this was that he had actually let himself fall in love with her again. He had wanted to rescue her when he saw her and Josh stranded. He had wanted to help her when she broke down crying at the diner. He had wanted to make her happy, to make her life better. What a fool he had been! Because all the while he was thinking about that, she was lying right to his face with little care about what she was doing.

Still, guilt gnawed at him as he placed the last of his belongings in the back of the truck bed. Before he had known about Josh, no one could have blamed him for not being apart of his son's life, but now he did know about Josh. If he just ran off and left him, what kind of father would that make him? He frowned and smacked the side of his truck before climbing in. Someday, Josh would understand...If Sarah ever even bothered to tell the kid the truth about who his dad really was that is.

CHAPTER FIFTEEN

"Sarah, please, reconsider," Henry begged as she came out to her CRV with another box full of stuff. "Just because Cade left, that's no reason for you to leave too."

She shook her head. "I'm sorry, Henry, but I told you when I started here that it was only going to be temporary. I just needed to save enough to get me and Josh started somewhere else, and I have."

"But why leave?" Henry protested, "You're doing so well as the cook, and Josh loves it here."

"Yea, but I can't stay," she declared, dropping the box off in the trunk, "There's too much of him here. I'd just be reminded of Cade every time I turned around."

"Sarah, give him time," Henry pleaded, "He'll come to his senses."

She shook her head. "Nope, he made himself crystal clear last night. I was a fool to think he'd changed."

Henry sighed. "Well, I've been praying for you two."

She smiled at that. "Thank you. That's sweet of you, but I'm fine... Really. I don't need Cade Jacobs in my life. Everything just gets so much more complicated when he's around."

"That's what love is, Darling," Emmie called as she walked up with a plastic dish in her hands, "Here's some cookies I baked for you and Josh. I thought you guys might enjoy some treats if you're really set on leaving. Traveling always makes me snackish."

Sarah's smile widened as she took the tub. "Thanks! Josh is going to love this."

"Have you told him yet?" Emmie asked.

Sarah cringed slightly. "I told him this morning before school. He didn't take it too well, but he'll be fine."

"I really wish you'd reconsider," Emmie stated, "You two are such a nice fit around here."

"I'm sorry, but I just can't," she replied, "You guys really should hate me anyway."

"Hate you? Why?" Emmie exclaimed.

"Well, I accidentally ran Cade off, and you two were the ones telling me all about what an excellent foreman he was and how this place couldn't get along without him before," she explained.

"Yes, he is, but he'll come back when he comes to his senses," Henry informed her, and Sarah wished she had his confidence.

Giving her an understanding look, Emmie smiled at her. "We don't blame you for all of this, Sarah. Cade's an adult, and he's allowed to make his own decisions. He just did what he thought was best for him, even if I do think he's making a big mistake." Then, crossing her arms, Emmie continued, "So, there's no reason for you to make the same mistake either. Why don't you reconsider sticking around?"

Sarah smiled at that but shook her head. "I'm sorry, but I can't. I've failed with Cade twice now, and I'm not going to stick around to make it three times."

"But maybe you should just give him time," Emmie countered, "It's a big shock learning you're a father."

"I don't think time's what he needs." Sarah shrugged. "Cade's made his position pretty clear, and I'll respect it."

"Well, if there's no talking you out of this," Emmie clicked her tongue. "Then, I guess all I have to say is I'll miss you two, and I'll be praying for you both every night. Be safe out there, and stay in touch." Emmie hugged her tightly, and Sarah smiled returning the hug. Being around Emmie made her miss her own mother. She was so kind and warm. Sarah was going to miss Emmie too.

Next, Henry gave her a quick hug goodbye and stated, "Stay in touch, you hear? And if you need anything—anything—you just let us know, okay?"

She laughed slightly even as her eyes pooled full of tears. "Thank you both for everything! It means a lot to me."

Then, shaking her head and swiping away at her tears, she stated, "Well, I've cried, even though I was sure I wouldn't. So, I'd better get going before—" Her voice trailed off as she shut her trunk. Before what? Before she changed her mind... Before she cried so much she couldn't leave... Before Cade reconsidered and came back to her... She shook her head. That last one was never going to happen. "I'll be seeing you guys around," she called with a wave of her hand. "Thanks again for everything."

"Goodbye, Sarah," Emmie replied, waving her hand quickly, "Safe travels."

"Take care of yourself," Henry stated, "And remember what I said."

She nodded as she started to climb into her car. "I will. Bye, guys."

And with that, she slipped into her car and shut the door on this chapter in her life. She sighed as she started the car and grabbed the steering wheel.

"Well, God, where to now?" she asked quietly as she pulled out of the drive.

As Cade drove down the highway, he struggled to keep Sarah out of his thoughts. Why was it so hard not to think about her? He hadn't slept well in the motel last night. Every time he closed his eyes, he was forced to relive a part of their argument or another time they had hung out. He frowned, his grip tightening on the steering wheel. The thing that was really getting to him was all the what if's. What if he hadn't left all those years ago? What if he and Sarah had worked their problems out in a mature way? He figured that they probably would have ended up getting married, and then Josh would never have been someone else's kid. He sighed. But that wasn't how it had happened. They hadn't been able to work things out. Their differences had been just too far apart...Just like they were this time. However, that thought got him thinking even more.

Yes, Sarah had lied to him, but she had also told him the truth when she hadn't had to. She could have gone on forever without telling him about Josh. Sure, maybe someday Cade would have put two and two together, but there was no guarantee of that. She had known how it was going to effect their relationship, but she had still told him the truth anyway. What had she stood to gain by telling him the truth? He had been hurt by the lie, hurt by all the time he had missed with his son, but was his way any better? He wasn't going to see Josh again...Or Sarah. Sure, she had made some mistakes, but so had he. Grace had covered over all of his sins, and in the Bible, when it talked about forgiveness, it said to forgive others like God had forgiven you. Cade frowned as he felt a pang of guilt. He hadn't been very forgiving to Sarah. He'd been stubborn and hardheaded. Just because she hadn't done it the way he would have, he'd reamed her out. He frowned. How did he know he wouldn't have made the same choices that she had had he been in her shoes? He didn't know what it was like to be her in that moment. It had to have been scary... At least, she had kept the baby, even if she had lied about who his parents were.

As he drove, he began to pray and pour his heart out to God. He told Him everything. He shared with him the pain he felt and the heartache. He told Him about how he had come to love Sarah again and the son he had never known he had. He prayed until there wasn't anything left to say, and he still prayed, pleading with God for guidance and help in this situation.

The longer he prayed, the more he felt like he was running away, and the less appealing the rodeo seemed. Still, fear nagged at him. Would Sarah even listen to him if he tried to talk with her again? What would have happened if he'd have turned back years ago? What would happen now if he did?

Suddenly, he felt a peace wash over him as he realized what he wanted to do. He needed to talk with Sarah again. He wanted to be a part of Josh's life, but he didn't want to lie to him. Maybe they could work out a compromise or something. He shook his head as he turned down the first exit he came to. It wasn't just Josh's life he wanted to be a part of though. He and Sarah had missed out on ten years because they had both been too stubborn to admit they were wrong. He didn't want another ten years to go by before he could finally tell her how much he loved her.

He'd been a stubborn fool, and he'd walked out and left Sarah Makenna for a second time in his life. He frowned. He just hoped she was willing to listen to him when he got back to the ranch. He may have already blown his chance. He sighed and once more took his problems to God praying, "Please, God, give me another chance. I'm sorry. I was just so angry, and I was afraid too. But You brought Sarah and Josh back into my life for a reason. You gave me a second chance, and I blew it. Please, help me fix this. I can't lose her again. I can't lose either of them."

With that, he got off the exit and turned around heading back for the ranch, hoping and praying he wasn't too late to make things right.

Sarah swiped at another stray tear as she and Josh drove out of Hopetown and headed for the bigger city of Orville. There was a diner there that needed a cook. Her shoulders slumped as she thought of the new job. The whole reason why she had given up her business is because she had wanted flexibility so she could spend more time with Josh, but she needed a job. She had tried the ranch life again, and it had just ended up breaking her heart once more. She shook her head. Never again.

"Why do we have to leave, Aunt Sarah?" Josh asked from the backseat. "I like it here."

"So, do I," she admitted quietly.

"Then, why are we leaving?" Josh pressed.

"Because—" she hesitated, not sure what to tell him. "Because we have to."

"But I didn't even get to say goodbye to Cade," Josh pouted.

"I already told you. He left last night. He was already gone," she informed him, "You couldn't have said bye to him."

"But why would he leave without saying goodbye?" Josh argued, "He was supposed to teach me how to ride horses."

"I don—" She shook her head. "I'm sure he had his reasons. I guess he was going to join the rodeo again," she countered, "Maybe he needed to leave right away for that."

"He still could have said bye," Josh protested, crossing his arms, "He was mad at us, wasn't he?"

"He's not mad at you," she informed him.

He considered this. "Well, why's he still mad at you when you went to talk with him? You said you were going to work it out so he'd still teach me. You didn't say he was going to leave!"

"I know, Josh, and I'm sorry," she offered quickly, "But I tried my best to get him to stay. I just couldn't."

"What's Cade so mad about?" he pressed.

"Well, I—I guess I lied to him a long time ago, and when I told him the truth, he got angry with me."

"Why'd you lie, Aunt Sarah?" Josh asked, sounding truly perplexed, "You always tell me not to lie."

She nodded. "I know, and I mean it. I guess I was just scared."

"Scared of what?"

"Scared of things," she replied vaguely, "But I'd hoped Cade would be able to understand why I had done it. I'd thought maybe he would see that I'd just been afraid, and he had to know how hard it had been for me to tell him the truth. But none of that mattered to him."

"Well, Aunt Sarah, he still could change his mind. He's a good guy," Josh pointed out, "You never know."

She chuckled at his youthful hope, but she shook her head. "No, Josh. I've been down this road before. Cade doesn't turn around. He's too stubborn. Once his mind's made up that he's going to do something, then that's what he does. It's too late for us."

Josh frowned and scratched his chin. "Maybe I should talk to him," he muttered more to himself than to her.

She had to try very hard to hide her smile from him. She could tell he was serious, and she was touched by the offer. But she knew it wouldn't change anything. Cade was not the type to change course.

"I am sorry, Josh, that it turned out this way," she replied once more swiping at a stray tear.

"It's okay, Aunt Sarah," Josh reassured her, "Don't cry."

So, he'd seen her tears even when she had tried to hide them. She should have known since he was so clever that she couldn't fool him for long. She forced a laugh and smiled up at him in the rear-view mirror.

"I'm okay," she informed him, and Josh nodded his head, believing her. It wasn't exactly a lie. She would be okay someday...Just right at this moment, she didn't feel so okay, but she would get over it. People do all the time...Get over a broken heart, she reassured herself.

But why, God, did it have to hurt so much?

Cade pulled up to Sarah's cabin and put his truck in park. Now that he was here, he suddenly hesitated. What was he going to say? Would she even bother to listen to him? He frowned as doubt needled at him, but he shook his head. With a prayer for strength and for the right words to say, he threw open his truck door and hurried up to her cabin, skipping the two steps that led to the porch in his haste.

He knocked on the door and glanced at his watch. It was almost three o'clock. Surely, she hadn't started cooking supper yet. Maybe she was still cleaning up from lunch. He blew out a breath and knocked again.

"Sarah, it's me! I need to talk to you!" he called.

No answer.

"Please, Sarah! I was wrong! Let's talk!"

Still nothing.

He blew out a disgruntled breath and raked his hands through his hair, but he knew he couldn't blame her if she didn't want to see him again. He didn't know what he had expected driving all the way back here. She had tried to bare her feelings to him, and he had slapped them away. He had been so stubborn, so sure he was right and she was wrong. He wouldn't blame her if she never talked to him again, but it would still break his heart.

"Sarah left this morning," Matt's voice informed him from behind.

Cade whipped around to face him. "Where did she go?"

"I don't know," Matt replied, "But I think she talked with Emmie and Henry before she left. Maybe they know something."

"Thanks, Matt," Cade stated, giving him a nod, "I'll go ask them then."

"Don't mention it," Matt said. Then, giving him a confused look, he added, "Hey, I thought you and Sarah hated each other now. What happened?"

"Turns out we just love each other is all," Cade informed him with a smile as he hurried around his pickup and headed for Henry's house.

He prayed he wasn't too late to fix things with Sarah as he ran, and he prayed Henry would know where she was. He wasn't sure what he was going to do if he didn't.

"What are you doing back?" a familiar voice

asked from over to his right, stopping him in his tracks. He whipped around to see Henry standing there feeding a burrow some carrot sticks. He patted the donkey on the head before wiping off his hands and turning to face Cade fully. "What's happened?"

"I changed my mind," Cade explained, "I need to find Sarah. I can't leave her again."

"Even though she lied to you?" Henry pressed, raising up an eyebrow.

He nodded. "We've both made some mistakes, and I was wrong. I don't agree with what she did, but I can understand it."

"So, you really want to make things right with her?" Henry asked.

"More than anything," Cade informed him.

"Well then, young sir, follow me," Henry ordered with a mischievous smile. "Someone had a hunch this was going to happen."

Cade shot him a confused look and was about to ask him what he meant, but Henry just held up a hand and stated, "Just follow me if you want to make things right with her."

"But I thought she left?"

"She did." Henry shrugged. "Now, come on.

You're wasting time."

Cade had to chuckle as he followed behind Henry. Maybe it was the stress that was getting to him or the weird way Henry was acting. Whatever it was, he just couldn't help it. He had to laugh, but on the inside, he still felt all torn up. Where was Sarah? Would he ever find her and Josh again? He'd royally messed up this time. He just prayed God could fix it.

CHAPTER SIXTEEN

S arah blew out a frustrated breath and checked through her suitcase once again.

"What's the matter, Aunt Sarah?" Josh asked, from his perch on the motel bed.

"I can't find my Bible," she replied, shaking her head. She had searched through everything she had brought from the ranch at least twice over now, and still she hadn't found it. But there was no way she would have left it behind. That Bible was her most precious treasure. It had all her notes and thoughts scribbled into it. Verses that had spoken to her were either highlighted, underlined, or circled. That Bible was like a diary to her. She would not have haphazardly lost it. She raked her hands through her hair. What was she going to do now?

"Maybe you left it at the ranch?" Josh offered,

"We could go back to check."

"No," she replied quickly, "It's too far to go back. It'd be a waste of time. I'm sure it's around here somewhere."

"Maybe you could call them," Josh pointed out, and Sarah perked up at the idea.

Maybe she could.

"That's a great idea, Josh," she informed him as she fished out her cellphone. "Once I rule out the ranch, then I'll know it has to be here somewhere!"

He nodded. "Or we can go back there to get it!" he stated a little too excitedly.

How was she going to get him on board with this whole leaving thing? Shaking her head, she dialed in Emmie's number and waited for her to pick up.

"Hello, Emmie?" she asked once the phone was answered.

"Sarah dear, is something the matter?" Emmie inquired, sounding concerned.

"No, well, I mean—I can't find my Bible, and while I was looking for it, Josh said I may have left it at the ranch, and he thought maybe I should call you," she informed her, "So, I figured I would just call to prove to both of us that I didn't leave it."

"Oh, well, I'm sorry to have to tell you this, Sarah, but you did leave it," Emmie explained, "Henry found it shortly after you left."

"What?! But I know I packed it," Sarah replied, shaking her head, "How could this happen?"

Then, a thought struck her, and she turned to face Josh, who was looking away from her and fiddling with the comforter on the bed.

"Josh?" she asked.

"Yea, Aunt Sarah?" Josh squeaked out.

"Did you do something back at the ranch with my Bible?" she pressed.

"Umm...well..." Josh hesitated, "I might have looked at it."

"And you didn't put it back?" Sarah demanded and shook her head. "Now, what am I going to do?"

"We could go get it!" Josh pointed out quickly.

"Yea, Henry and I will make sure nothing happens to it until you arrive," Emmie added, and Sarah realized she was still on the phone.

"No, I don't think we should," Sarah informed them both, "Can you just send it to me?"

"Oh, well, I suppose," Emmie stuttered.

"But Aunt Sarah!" Josh protested, "It's your

Bible! You don't go anywhere without it!"

"We can't go back now," Sarah argued, "We'll lose so much time."

"You know what they say," Emmie countered, "God's delays are His protection."

Sarah blew out a breath, knowing Emmie was right. Sometimes, God did do things differently from our plans, but Sarah also suspected that Josh had had something to do with this. She frowned at him, but he simply shrugged innocently.

"So? Are we going to go back?" he asked.

She sighed and nodded her head. "I guess we are."

"Yippee!" Josh exclaimed, jumping up to his feet and pumping his arms in the air.

"But we aren't staying," Sarah quickly reminded him, and Josh nodded his head.

"I know," he answered, surprising her. If he had had something to do with this, that wasn't exactly the answer she had expected.

"Alright, we'll be watching for you two," Emmie replied, once again reminding Sarah she was still on the phone, "See you soon."

And with that, Emmie actually hung up. Sarah

shook her head, unable to understand all of this.

What are You trying to show me, God? She prayed silently as she threw her things back into her suitcase.

As soon as Sarah put the CRV in park, Josh flew out of the car and raced over to Fantasma's corral talking softly to her as she timidly approached him.

"Josh, don't wander off," she called over to him, "I'm just going to get my Bible, and then we need to leave again."

"Ahh...Do we have to?" Josh whined as he stroked the horse's nuzzle.

Sarah sighed. This is why she hadn't wanted to come back here. She shook her head as she walked up to Emmie and Henry's house. She didn't bother arguing with him now. There would be plenty of time for that later when they were actually ready to leave. She knocked and stood there waiting for one of them to answer the door.

When Emmie finally came to the door, she smiled and pointed to the barn. "Henry left your Bible on the shelf in the office in there."

"In the barn?" Sarah wasn't sure how to take that.

Surely, they knew how important that was to her. Why would they leave it in the barn of all places? But she decided to give them the benefit of the doubt. She had said it was in the office. Maybe it was safe there anyway.

Emmie nodded, and Sarah smiled. "Okay, thanks."

She walked towards the barn, shaking her head. Something about that conversation just seemed odd. Emmie just didn't seem like herself. What was going on here?

When she rounded the corner, however, she had to take a step back as her breath caught in her throat. Cade stood there with her Bible in his hands and with that smile of his that he seemed to only give to her on his face.

"Hi," he offered.

"What are you doing here?!" she demanded. It was the only question of the millions racing around her mind that she could actually catch.

He frowned and looked down briefly before locking eyes with her. "I got to thinking about how different our lives would have been ten years ago if I hadn't left. You, Josh, and I would've been able to have been a family. There wouldn't have been any lies or resentment between us." He inhaled sharply before continuing. "Then I realized that I was making the same mistake again. God had given me a second chance, and I was blowing it again because I was too stubborn to see it."

Tears welled in her eyes at his words, and she put a hand up to her mouth. She had never thought she would hear Cade admit any of this.

"I love you, Sarah Makenna. I know I've messed up. We both have," he offered, "But I think we can make it if we try."

"Even though I lied?" she pressed skeptically.

He nodded as he approached her and handed her her Bible. His hands lingered on hers and he said, "You once told me that fear had held you back in our relationship, but you were done being afraid. Well, I'm done being so pigheaded."

The admission made her laugh even as tears streamed down her cheeks.

"I know I can be stubborn," he replied, "But I want to do better. I realized that I can't lose you guys now. I love you both so much, and you're a part of my life now. I can't imagine never seeing you again or hearing your laugh or seeing Josh grow up."

"Even if Josh still thinks of me as his aunt and you just as Cade?" she asked.

He flashed her a mischievous smile. "Well, I've been thinking about that, and I'll explain it in more detail in a minute. But first, there's something I need to ask you."

Before she could ask what he meant, he pulled out a ring from his back pocket, and he knelt down on one knee.

"Sarah, will you marry me?" he asked, and she felt like someone had knocked the wind right out of her lungs.

Her brain felt like it was spinning, and she shook her head. What was going on here? "But I thought—"

"I am sorry, Sarah, about what I said the other night," he added, "Can we try again?"

"I—I don't know..." She shook her head somberly. "It might take a long, long time for my heart to handle trying us again..."

His face fell, and his eyes were sad. But to his credit, he nodded his head. "I understand."

"Then, again..." She gave him a sweet smile, and his eyes lit up. "The way I figure it, we both messed this relationship up. If you can forgive me, I think I can forgive you."

His shoulders relaxed slightly, and he smiled.

"Now, about your other question," she continued, and his shoulders immediately stiffened again. She tenderly placed a hand on his face. "Yes."

"What?" His face paled slightly, but his eyes lit up with excitement.

"I'm saying yes to marrying you. We were engaged once before," she stated with a shrug. "It shouldn't be that much of a shock."

He shook his head. "I never thought I would ever hear you say that again though."

She smiled teasingly at him. "I'm full of surprises I guess."

"So, am I," he replied, pulling her into his arms and kissing her soundly on the lips.

It felt so good to be in his arms again. To melt into his embrace. Everything else seemed to vanish around them. Sure, she knew life wasn't going to be perfect. She wasn't going to be able to control everything that happened, but she was okay with that now. She was tired of having fear control her life, and the fact that Cade had come here and done what he did proved to her he was going to be different too. They were finally going to be a family. She had longed for this day so much when she was just a teenager and head over heels in love with him, but then, she had buried that dream after their breakup. Now though, here in his arms, that dream roared back to life, burning bright with hope, and she was thrilled at the prospect of becoming his wife.

"Okay," he stated, pulling slightly away from her, and she missed his warmth immediately, "Now, that I've gotten that question out of the way. I have another important question for you."

"What?" she asked, her heart sinking. What was this about?

"I was just wondering if the three of us are going to be a family anyway, how about we adopt Josh?" he asked.

"What? But Josh is—"

He stopped her question with a smile that said he knew what she was going to say.

"If we legally adopt Josh, he'll be our son officially. We won't have to lie to him anymore, and yet he won't lose his parents either. He'll have the best of both worlds, right?"

New tears sprang to her eyes, and she nodded her head quickly as she began to cry.

"You mean that?" she asked.

He nodded. "I wouldn't have said it if I didn't mean it," he informed her, pulling her into a hug again. "I want us to be a family...A real family." He rubbed her back gently, tenderly as she tried to stop her tears.

"So," he asked, peering down at her, "What do you say?"

"I say yes!" she exclaimed, swiping away the last of her tears. "Cade Jacobs, you are a genius!"

"Well, I am pretty smart," he teased, "But I don't know if I'd say—"

She stopped his protests with a kiss, and he pulled her closer.

"Did you guys make up or what?" Josh asked from the doorway.

His words pulled her back into reality as she realized he was standing there staring at them, and she reluctantly pulled away, ending the kiss, though she missed the warmth of Cade's lips the second she did. She, however, smiled at Josh and nodded her head.

"We did," she replied, "We're going to get married!"

"Yipppeee!" Josh exclaimed, rushing over to them, "I knew my plan would work!"

"What plan?" Sarah asked.

"I gave Henry your Bible before we left so we'd have to come back," Josh informed her.

"You did what?" she exclaimed.

He nodded. "I knew you were upset about Cade, and I wanted to try and fix things somehow. But I knew I couldn't fix things if we left," he replied as if it were obvious, "So, I gave Henry the Bible that way we would have to come back here."

"But how did you know Cade would be here?" she pressed.

"I didn't," Josh admitted with a boyish shrug, "But I prayed he would be, and he was."

She smiled wide at that and pulled him into a hug. "So, I take it you're alright with us becoming a family, Josh?" she asked as she glanced up at Cade.

Josh nodded his head. "Of course! I like Cade a lot," he informed her, "And now, he'll have to finish teaching me how to ride horses."

At that, Cade laughed and smiled. "I guess I will."

"And you know what else?" Sarah asked, pulling Josh's attention back to her, "Cade and I are going to adopt you."

Josh's eyes got as big as saucers. "So that means

Cade's going to get to be my dad?!"

She glanced up at Cade with a knowing look in her eye and nodded. "Yea, that makes him your dad."

"Yes!" Josh threw his arms around them both and hugged them tightly.

Then, as he stood back to look at them again, he asked, "So, we get to stay on the ranch now too, right? And I don't have to leave my school again?"

She nodded. "Yep, on both counts."

"This is the best day ever!" Josh declared, throwing his head back and spinning in a circle.

"I think I've got to agree with him," Cade declared, leaning in close and kissing her forehead, "I love you, Sarah Makenna."

"And I love you, Cade Jacobs."

She stood on her tiptoes and brushed a kiss against his lips. They had both made their mistakes. They had both ruined their relationship in the past, but now—now, they had both grown and matured. And she had a feeling they would be just fine.

"Hey, Josh, how about we start your horse riding lessons again?" Cade asked him, and Sarah smiled as she watched Josh's face light up.

"You mean it?" Josh exclaimed, his eyes huge.

Cade nodded, and Sarah smiled wide.

Josh's smile grew bigger, and he jumped into the air. "Yippee!"

Sarah relaxed as she leaned her head on Cade's shoulder and watched Josh celebrate. Ten years ago, before they had broken up, this had been everything she had hoped their life would be like. The two of them together with their kids. But then, life and fears and anger had gotten in the way, and she had never wanted to see him again. She had thought this dream was dead and buried, but God had had other plans. He had known what was best for them, and He had given them both time to grow into the people they were supposed to be before bringing them together again. Even though it had been hard, it had been totally worth it, she realized as she glanced up at Cade and smiled softly,. They were together now, all three of them, and that made it totally worth it.

EPILOGUE

One Year later...

"Josh, it's time to eat!" Sarah called from the porch of her and Cade's two story farmhouse that was located on its own part of the Wild Hearts Ranch. It was a beautiful home, and they had made it theirs over the course of this last year.

"In a minute!" Josh called as he turned in his saddle and moved Fantasma around to once again practice the barrel run that Cade had set up for him to train on for competitions.

"Josh..." Her tone was firmer this time.

"Just once more, Mom. Pleasssseeeee....."

She smiled. Even though it had been several months since Josh's adoption had been finalized and since he had decided on his own to call them Mom and Dad, it still took her by surprise every time she heard him call her that. It never failed to make her smile. She had thought she had lost her chance for him to call her that when she had given him up years ago, but thankfully, God had had other plans about that too.

"Alright," she replied, "One more round, but then that's it. You've got to eat something."

He smiled wide and dashed off on his horse. After Cade had tamed Fantasma all the way, Henry had given him to Josh since the horse had seemed to take such a liking to him, and the two of them had been practically inseparable ever since.

Suddenly, Hannah began to fuss in her bassinet, and Sarah went over to her and gave her back the binky she had let fall from her mouth into her lap.

"Shhhh...you're all right," she soothed her and Cade's two month old daughter. She smiled to herself at that. Life had happened so fast since that moment a year ago in the barn when she and Cade were reunited. They hadn't waited long to get married. It had only taken a couple of weeks to get everything ready, and since Henry was the pastor that was going to perfume the ceremony, they had gotten a church and everything fast too. They hadn't figured they had needed a long engagement since they had been engaged once before. So, they'd had a small wedding with her mother, Henry and Emmie, and all the ranch hands in attendance in the old, white, steepled church located in the center of Hope Town. It had been beautiful. After the honeymoon, they'd moved into the new house that Henry had set up for her and Cade, and several months later, they had figured out sweet little Hannah was on the way. Life sure had a way of changing drastically in no time flat.

Just then, someone came up from behind her and wrapped his arms around her, kissing her on the cheek.

"Good morning, Mrs. Jacobs," Cade stated as he held her tight.

She smiled and leaned into his embrace, enjoying the comfort of his warmth around her. "You're late for lunch," she teased.

He smirked at her as he kissed her. "Am I late now?"

"Alright, you'll get just a warning this time," she replied smugly, "I'll let you off the hook for now."

"I knew you'd see it my way," he informed her as he kissed her cheek and smiled.

She laughed and waved him off as she turned to

get the food on the table, and he then turned his attention to the baby.

"And how's my other favorite girl this morning?" he asked as he picked Hannah up.

"Fussy," Sarah replied as she sat the chicken salad on the table.

"Oh, that's just 'cause she's missing her daddy, isn't it sweetheart?" he asked gently bouncing her in his arms. Then, turning towards where Josh was practicing, he called, "Good job, Buddy! I think you're going to give 'em a run for their money at the next show!"

"Thanks!" Josh called back, waving from his horse.

"Alright, Josh, it's time to eat," she informed him as she set the buns and chips out too, "Come on up now."

"I will! Just let me put Fantasma out to pasture!" Josh informed her.

She rolled her eyes and shook her head. That boy...She just couldn't get him off that horse for nothing. Then, she caught sight of Cade standing there cuddling the baby, and she felt her heart nearly melt in her chest. He had grown so much since that night they had ended their engagement years ago, and he had become the man she loved wholeheartedly, desperately, and completely.

He glanced over and caught her staring, and he gave her a lopsided grin. "What?" he asked.

"Oh, nothing." She shrugged. "I was just thinking."

"Thinking about what?"

"You...Me...Everything," she replied.

"We have come a long way," he agreed, nodding his head.

"A lot has changed," she added.

He kissed Hannah's sleeping head and smiled at her. "For the better."

"Yep, for the better," she agreed.

Just then, Josh came racing up and slid into his seat at the table. "Where's the food?" he asked, "I'm starving!"

"Wait one second, young man. Did you wash your hands?" she demanded.

He nodded. "At the wash station by the stable."

"Alright, then." She gave him a smile and a kiss on the head. "That's my boy."

Then, taking the lid off the chicken salad, she dished a sandwich up for each member of her family. Her family...She had never dreamed she would be able to say that. She had thought her chances for a family had passed her bye, but God had had other plans for her life. Now, she was full. She was complete, and she had Him solely to thank for it.

As she looked around the table, her heart swelled with love, and she thanked God for each one of them. She knew whatever came their way they would be able to handle it because this time both Cade and Sarah were putting God first. He was a part of their daily lives, and she knew that He was the ultimate one responsible for getting the two of them back together. She smiled as a hummingbird flew by the deck looking to get some nectar from her Rose of Sharon bushes. God had been so good to her and blessed her so much. She had the family she had always hoped for and dreamed of. What more could she want? Life was good...

Dear Reader,

I hope you enjoyed Sarah and Cade's journey as they were forced to reunite and try to figure out what that meant for them. Their story was one I really enjoyed writing, and I'm hoping to bring them and their family back in future books in this series.

While it took Cade and Sarah ten years to find their second chance, sometimes, second chances aren't always possible. Sometimes, we feel like we get one shot, and that's it. Sometimes, reconciliation never happens, and relationships are lost forever. But I want to reassure you that God loves giving second chances. No matter what you have done, He wants to welcome you with open arms if only you would repent and turn to Him. You can never run too far or fall so low that He will not be able to save you. Just call out to Jesus, and He will answer. God loves you so very much.

I hope to release the next book in this series, The Cowgirl's Second Chance, soon. I'm shooting for early spring of next year. So, be watching for it!

If you enjoyed this book, please consider leaving a review and letting me and others know about it. That really helps me out! Thank you for joining me on this journey and for supporting an indie author like me. It is my dream to make a living as an author and to be able to do it full time. So, every sale, every review, and every follow is much appreciated because it puts me one step closer to my goal. Thank you again! Have a blessed day!

Sincerely,

Kayla Freshcorn

A country girl with a broken heart comes back home to find a second chance at love with a man she would never have expected.

Read on for a sneak preview of The Cowgirl's Second Chance...

Rebecca finished drying off her hair and headed to her computer dressed in her favorite pair of sweats. A sense of dread came over her as she opened the laptop and clicked on her email.

Nate was right. She needed to know what was in the email. The what if's were driving her crazy, and it was probably nothing serious at all. She was likely making a mountain out of a molehill. She sat down, tucking her leg underneath her as she waited on the email program to boot up. Once it had, she leaned forward and clicked on Edward's email.

She held her breath as she hastily scanned every line.

"Rebecca, I made a mistake giving up all of my rights to our daughter. I was young…" She scoffed. Not that much time had passed. "I was under the influence when I sent you and her away. You know how I had a problem with alcohol before, but I got treated for it. I'm fine now, and Gracie needs a father. Now, I want to be a part of her life. We both know I can give her a much better life than you ever could. So, just do us both a favor and give her to me. You can keep acting on the stage or whatever it is you're doing now, and she will grow up surrounded by the best of everything. When you think about it...it would honestly be selfish of you to keep her from me. Are you going to be that selfish? Are you going to try and keep her from having the best in life?"

Rebecca's blood ran cold as she read the words, and she could almost see him standing there telling her all these things in his condescending way. Why was he wanting to take Gracie from her all of the sudden? Was it genuinely because he just wanted to be a part of her life? Then, why did he want her to give up custody of Gracie? Was it to hurt Rebecca? Possibly. Her hands trembled as she read on in the email.

"If you try to keep me from seeing her, I will fight you in court, and what judge would choose you over me. Remember, all the judges around here know my dad. Just make this easy on both of us."

She couldn't read anymore. She slammed the laptop closed and leaned her head back against the couch cushions. *Why God? Why is he doing this now? What is he really after?*

Tears rolled down her cheeks as she prayed, but just then, Gracie began to fuss, and she swiped away her tears as a new resolve filled her very being. She stood up and crossed the room to the crib, knowing what she had to do. She would fight Edward with everything she had. Even if it cost her everything, she would fight him. There was no way she would leave her daughter with him. After all, what would happen to her once he got bored with being a dad? Would he just dump her in a boarding school or abandon her with his parents or Rebecca again a few years from now? No, she wouldn't let that happen.

She picked Gracie up and got ready to feed her. She would give her the best life she could possibly give her. No matter what.

Made in the USA
Monee, IL
03 January 2025

76018097R00164